I0638488

THE MEMORY HUNTER

Special Agent O'Malley, FBI

By

Colin Setterfield

COPYRIGHT

Copyright © 2016 Colin Setterfield

ALL RIGHTS RESERVED

This ebook is licensed for your personal enjoyment only. This ebook may not be re-sold or given away to other people. If you would like to share this book with another person, please purchase an additional copy for each recipient. If you're reading this book and did not purchase it, or it was not purchased for your use only, then please return to your favorite ebook retailer and purchase your own copy. Thank you.This ebook is a work of fiction. Names, characters, businesses, organizations, places, events, and incidents either are the product of the author's imagination or are used fictitiously. Any resemblance

to actual persons, living or dead, events, or locale is entirely coincidental

ISBN 978-1-988719-10-8

Content

Prologue

Bob turned off the recorder and leaned back in his chair. The listening device on Gracie Beauchamp's phone had served him well and he knew what had to be done. A quick reflection on the anonymous letters brought a lump to his throat. When all appeared to be going so well, the inevitable curve ball sailed over the plate, to threaten the viability of his future.

Gracie's younger sister, Veronica, a waitress at the Flashpoint nightclub in lower Manhattan, became the first casualty of this blackmail endeavor. On a one-night stand two weeks earlier, an inebriated Bob let slip a clue regarding his dilemma—words Veronica should never have heard. He could not risk anyone finding out the truth and the girl had to go.

Her laptop revealed no evidence of their night together, or any connection between the two of them, but the possibility of a diary came to mind. Bob searched her apartment but couldn't find anything. The next morning, Gracie's appearance in the wake of her sister's

death cautioned him into following Gracie home, and at a later time, bugging her phone.

The recording of her call to the local police precinct confirmed his suspicions with regard to the younger sister, Veronica, having kept a journal. Lieutenant Dunmore would pick it up from Gracie's apartment at around 5:30 p.m. Bob needed to get there ahead of Dunmore and make sure the diary did not fall into police hands.

He glanced at his watch—4:05 p.m. Gracie would be home by 5:00. Sadness crept over him. But for one mistake, things could have been so different.

∞∞

1

A Heartbreaking Discovery

Lieutenant Dunmore closed the door to the apartment and removed a cellphone from his pocket. Gracie Beauchamp lay on the hall floor, mouth slightly open in a grimace of shock. He had felt for vital signs and found her still alive. He immediately called 911. Twenty years in the force did not make the circumstance any easier for him. He doubted she would make it. Ten minutes later, the paramedics arrived and carted her off to the local hospital's emergency. Dunmore called his office and explained the scenario to his assistant.

"Arrange for a guard to be stationed at the general hospital for a Gracie Beauchamp, an attempted murder victim, who is on the way there by ambulance. I would hate the killer to realize she is still alive and try to finish the job."

The status of this case escalated with sudden perpetuity. First Veronica Beauchamp's murder; now her older sister Gracie, who had made mention of a presidential assassination plot as recorded in her sister's journal, might follow in her footsteps. Armed with this latest information, Dunmore knew he would have to bring in the FBI.

The phone rang a few seconds before a gruff voice answered. "Criminal Investigation, Special Agent O'Malley speaking."

"Good evening, Agent O'Malley—Lieutenant Dunmore, local, lower Manhattan Precinct"

"What can I do for you, Lieutenant?"

"I'm presently investigating a crime and need to report some information I received just prior to my arrival on the scene—which has now turned out to be an attempted murder."

"Why would it require the FBI, Lieutenant?"

"Because the victim shared a vital piece of information with me on the phone which I needed to verify, but she was attacked before I could get to her."

"....and the information?" asked O'Malley.

"A possible assassination attempt on the President of the United States."

After a brief hesitation, O'Malley responded. "That's interesting. Are you sure your source was of sound mind?"

"Her name is Gracie Beauchamp and she's a journalist with the Political Arrow. I first met her after her sister, Veronica, a waitress at the Flashpoint nightclub, was murdered two weeks ago. The story goes that Veronica met this guy named Bob at the nightclub and she took him back to her apartment in lower Manhattan for a nightcap. The guy was a bit pissed and apparently said something about involvement with a presidential assassination plot."

O'Malley absorbed the information. "How did the journalist get involved?"

"The journalist is the older sister, as I said. She got a call from her younger sister, Veronica, the next morning to say that this guy, Bob, told her to forget what he had said, that he was just a little drunk. He then left the apartment.

Veronica, according to Gracie the older sister, seemed scared—said the guy swore her to secrecy and if she spoke of the matter she would be harmed. Gracie felt apprehensive about the whole thing and decided to go to Veronica's apartment. When she got there, she found her sister dead."

O'Malley grunted his understanding. "So the older sister, Gracie—the journalist—called you guys?"

"You got it. I responded to that first investigation but couldn't find any clues as to the identity of the killer. Ten days later when the crime scene was decommissioned, Gracie went back to pack up her sister's belongings and that's when she came across a diary in the bookcase, which made specific mention of the incident."

O'Malley had the gist of things now. "So she took the diary home with her and called you, but the killer got there before you. My guess is the diary has disappeared?"

"I'm afraid so. I found a listening device on her phone. When I got here, Gracie was hanging

onto life. It doesn't look good—I don't think she's going to make it."

"I feel your pain," said O'Malley.

"We only have her verbal testimony regarding the potential assassination plot, so I don't know how you want to play it—an assassination is further up your alley than mine," ventured Dunmore.

"Give me both addresses and we'll look into that side of it while you continue to follow up on the murder and the assault," said O'Malley.

Dunmore gave the Special Agent the names, addresses, plus work details of both the girls and hung up. He looked around the apartment and discovered Gracie's car keys with an apartment key, which he removed. He locked the door and left for the hospital.

*

The nurse outside the operating theatre answered the lieutenant's inquiry with professional politeness. "She's still in the operating

room. You'll have to wait for the operating doctor to finish."

"Thanks, I'll wait." Dunmore sat on a sofa outside the theatre doors and picked up a magazine from the side table. He didn't feel like going back to the office and would head for home from the hospital at eight p.m, the end of his shift, if the doctor did not make an appearance by then. He turned the pages automatically and barely saw the print.

His mind still wanted to focus on the look of shock, registered on Gracie's face when he found her on the floor—a good-looking lass with a nice figure and a well-paying job. He would not have minded knowing her prior to the incident. He thought about his divorce, now in its fifth year, and the children he rarely got to see. It wasn't his ex-wife's fault. He had buried himself in work ever since; a way to cover his failure.

"Lieutenant?" The doctor stared down at him.

He jumped up and dropped the magazine. "How is she, Doctor—will she make it?"

The doctor held his gaze. "She's suffered a bad internal head injury and oxygen starvation. There's nothing more I can do for her. We will have to see. I'm afraid you'll not be able to question her—she's in a coma."

Dunmore nodded sadly. "I have arranged for a guard to be on duty outside her ward. If anything happens, either way, will you please have the receptionist call me on my cell?"

The doctor agreed and after Dunmore had given his cell number to the duty nurse, he left for home.

∞∞

2

Two Days Later

Lucas Wheeler, a professor at the New York Neuro Institute of Technology, turned and raised his eyebrows at the dean of the faculty. "Who wants to see me?"

The dean, a short, skinny man with large square-framed spectacles perched on the end of a bony-vein proliferated nose, raised his chin. "A guy—says he's from the FBI."

"Why would the FBI want to talk to me? I haven't done anything wrong—well, not recently, anyway."

Samantha Pink, Lucas's assistant chipped in, "You mean, not that you can remember."

Lucas frowned, looked thoughtfully at the floor for a moment and ran a hand through his long, blond, almost shoulder-length hair. "It must have to do with that article the Institute published on our project." He looked up at the dean and scowled. "I told you we should have waited."

The dean shot back. "Don't blame me—if we didn't produce some proof of your break-through, our funding for the project would have been in jeopardy."

"You don't even know if that's the reason why he's here to see you, Lucas," said Saman-tha. She scratched the side of her lip where a silver ring pierced the skin and adjusted her seat on the edge of Lucas's desk.

"Do you want me to send him away and perhaps you can see him on your own time?" said the dean.

"No—that won't be necessary. I'm sure it's nothing serious; send him to my office."

The dean scurried off, glad to get a decisive answer from Wheeler. His faculty professor, although brilliant, often displayed a reluctance to take direct responsibility for anything. One never knew if Lucas ever revealed the truth about his real feelings, unless it had to do with work. Life seemed to be one huge party for him and things that worried most people didn't appear to faze Wheeler at all. He acted more like an adolescent in a man's body.

Lucas turned to his assistant. "You'd better come as well, Sam."

Samantha smiled. She slid off the desk and grabbed his arm. "Is the good, little-old professor afraid of the big, bad FBI man?"

Lucas laughed and the two of them waltzed down the corridor from the lab to his office. Samantha, a slim girl of twenty-eight years lived up to her last name, Pink, with a sense of committed conformity. She took great care to emulate her favorite pop singer of the same name and christened her appearance with a spiky, pink colored hairdo.

The silver rings which pierced her lip, left eyebrow, and nose presented a challenge for most intellectuals to believe she actually held a responsible position in the Institute. Her funky appearance belied the intelligence which lay within the gray matter situated behind the sparkling blue eyes and the status of a competent neurophysicist seemed far from a reality. But competent she was. Lucas Wheeler would be the first to acknowledge her contribution to the Memory Sweep Project.

They all arrived at Lucas's office at the same time. The dean with the FBI agent in tow, stopped at the entrance to allow Lucas and Samantha in first, while he zipped into an adjacent office to acquire another chair. The dean introduced the agent, who shook both Wheeler's and Samantha's hands, before settling his lanky, six-foot frame in a seat.

"Special Agent O'Malley is here to enquire about the Memory Sweep Project you're working on."

Lucas looked at Samantha who acknowledged his implied sentiment of 'I told you so.'

O'Malley ran a hand through his dark, bushy hair and sized up the two scientists. He decided not to pass any judgements before he knew more about them. Impressions did, however, flash through his mind. He saw a hippy in his thirties and a funky, trendy, party girl, neither of whom matched the predisposed considerations of possible recipients of a Nobel Prize.

"I read about your breakthrough in the Science Monitor and I want to congratulate both of you for your outstanding work," said O'Malley.

Lucas smiled. "Thank you, Special Agent, however, I'm sure you didn't come here to sing our praises—as much as we appreciate your sentiments."

O'Malley shifted in his seat. "No, you're absolutely correct, Professor. Thank you for being so candid. I'm here because the FBI sees a great use for your breakthrough."

For a second, O'Malley's deep blue eyes focused on Samantha and she felt drawn to him. She liked the way his hair flowed back over the ears and formed a duck's tail at the back of his head. The tinges of gray, appearing at the temples gave him a dapper look, but the bushy eyebrows needed trimming—she would love to do it for him. "What sort of use?" she asked.

"Crime resolution," said O'Malley.

Lucas turned to the dean, who avoided his gaze by looking up at the ceiling.

"I'm not sure we actually had that in mind," said Lucas.

"What did you have in mind, then, Professor?"

Lucas hesitated. To be honest with himself, his thoughts on the matter of actual use for Memory Intrusion, had become totally eclipsed by the science of being able to do it—to be able to enter someone else's memory banks and actually see the resident memories. The question of how to use it would probably not be up to him, however, the agent asked an extremely poignant question.

"I've never really given the vast possible use of the memory sweep much thought. As you might appreciate, the science of just doing it, took all our mental efforts."

Samantha came to the rescue. "I have thought somewhat about the matter. I envisaged helping people, who through age or injury, had lost some of their memory. Perhaps also for those, who suffer amnesia due to trauma, or disease.

I think there are limitations for which the breakthrough should be used."

"What about solving a murder?" asked O'-Malley.

Lucas and Samantha both looked at the dean. He inclined his head and thought for a moment before offering a solution. "I realize there will be some privacy considerations and to answer your question, Special Agent O'Malley, I would venture to say that this is not a question we can answer for you right now. The breakthrough is the intellectual property of the Institute and my guess is the board would not condone it for such a use."

O'Malley narrowed his eyes. "I would have thought if your son or daughter was murdered and certain people carried vital information as to who the killer was, you would not hesitate to agree to the sweep's use."

The dean looked uncomfortable. "I understand where you are coming from, but there will be those who would not agree with you. Our funding, as a medical institute, is reliant on some very influential people and we could stand to lose a great deal of our financial base."

"Not if the government ordered you to do it. If this science really works, then it should work for the good of mankind. I could arrange for a judge to provide us with an injunction."

Lucas held up his hand to interject. "We are not even sure it will really work. There are some grave dangers for the investigator while lurking in a target's mind. The science is still theoretical, and although it works on paper, there's no telling if it will work in actual practice."

"Are you saying you use your own mind to investigate someone else's memory?"

"I won't go into the specifics—the article in the Science Monitor explains some of it, but yes, the investigator's mind is intricately involved in the process."

"Is there a danger to the target mind or brain?"

"Not that we know of specifically, but we can't be sure," said Lucas.

"Then, you'll need an experiment to seal the deal," said O'Malley.

Samantha turned to Lucas. "We do need to test out the equipment with a real live, human mind."

"I don't know. I never anticipated any conflict to accompany the project, but now I'm seeing all sorts of problems."

O'Malley grinned. "I have the ideal candidate, Dr. Wheeler. It's also an extremely worthwhile cause and I'm going to let you in on a secret which you cannot tell anyone else, beyond these walls—if you do, I'll have to kill you."

Intrigued by his words, the three scientists looked at one another, then nodded. They wanted to know what the FBI found so pressing, that intrusion into someone's memory, warranted the ethically-explosive experiment.

O'Malley proceeded to tell them about the saga which underpinned the potential assassination of the President of the United States. He told them everything he knew up to the moment.

"We only have a very limited window to solve this mystery—the proposition memory belongs to Gracie Beauchamp and she is only just hanging onto life. The doctors fear she might pass soon and I am assuming once the brain dies, the memory will die as well."

Astounded, the dean expressed his incredulity. "A girl has died and another is about to die because some criminal said something he shouldn't have?"

Samantha, also shocked to the core, sounded off in her potty-mouthed style. "Oh crap. What a freakin' sadist."

Lucas sat still and said nothing.

"So you can see why we want to solve this crime. In Gracie Beauchamp's memory is one very important image—the page of her sister's diary, in which there may be a description of the killer and confirmation of a potential plot to assassinate the President. She may also have seen her assailant's face."

Lucas stood to indicate he wanted the conversation to come to an end. "I am conflicted and it's not something I want to make a resolution on. I suggest you approach a judge and get your injunction. At this point, although, you have made a good argument for use of the sweep, I am not convinced it's legitimate for such a purpose."

The dean stood and stretched out his hand to O'Malley. "For now, I'm standing with Dr. Wheeler on this. I understand you want to solve a crime and save a president, who by the way is the most unpopular leader, America has ever voted into office."

O'Malley, a little peeved at their final prognosis, shook each hand in turn. "I understand your reluctance and I don't blame you for being hesitant. I'll speak to my superior and see if an injunction is what he would want to go for."

The dean saw O'Malley out. Lucas and Samantha stared at each other.

"I think you should have agreed to do it," she said.

Lucas scowled and remained in thought.

Samantha tried to press the point home. "I'm not against our work being used for solving such violent crimes. Just think if Gracie Beauchamp was your sister, or daughter."

"There is much more at stake here than the emotions of a distraught parent, Sam. I can see a host of privacy and moral issues, arising out of the sweep's use. I don't want to become the target of anti-science sentiment."

"Wimp," she teased.

"Not so," he countered.

She laughed and punched him on the shoulder, to which he responded with a playful shove. Samantha grabbed his wrist and pulled him toward her—their faces came into close quarters and they stared into each other's eyes. She found Lucas attractive but he never let on about his feelings for her. Every time they arrived at a point of physical contact he would break it off with a goofy saying—this incident would be no different.

He smiled and said, "I've just remembered something."

"What?"

"I left a tap running in the kitchen."

She giggled and shoved him away from her. That's how it always ended and inside she felt a distinct let-down. "Are you never capable of anything serious?" she asked.

"Only if it's scientific," he answered.

"Sometimes I think you're an idiot."

He grinned. "But at least I'm an educated idiot."

The dean returned and stood at the office door looking at them. "Are you two goofing off again?"

"Just relieving the tension," said Lucas.

"What did you really think about O'Malley's request?"

"As I said—I'm conflicted. I can only see problems for us if the sweep is used for such a purpose. Besides, they have always managed to solve most crimes without the use of such a device. I don't see why they should benefit from it now."

"As far as the President is concerned, they can go ahead and assassinate him—I don't give a damn, but I draw the line at the murder of two young women," said the dean.

"I agree one hundred percent, but old flip-flop here can only think about the morality of trespassing inside someone else's mind." Samantha gestured toward Lucas who stuck his tongue out at her.

The dean sighed. "You two belong in Kindergarten. We'll soon see what happens if that prick of a special agent gets his way."

"I liked him. He's kind of cute," said Samantha.

"He's married," said Lucas. "Ring on the finger."

She made a face and walked off.

∞∞

3

Dealing with Guilt and Emotion

O'Malley and his wife sat opposite each other at the dinner table. They ate in the usual silence.

"Penny for your thoughts?" asked Janet.

"Just thinking about the case I'm on."

"As always," she said. A hint of sarcasm found its way through the timbre of her voice.

He stopped and with slow deliberation put the knife and fork on his plate. "Okay—do you want to talk about it?"

"Anything which involves the subject of 'us,' always appears to get bogged down by you reluctance to follow through. I know you can't talk about your work—I realized this would be the case before I married you. I want to talk about us."

"What is it about us you want to discuss?"

Janet hesitated. "We can't seem to get by the problem of Fallon's death. It hangs over us like a funeral pyre. When are you going to stop blaming yourself and allow us to end our mourning?"

"A father holds his responsibility toward his daughter in a different way."

"Please, Dillon. I'm trying to understand. I am also in pain—but I discovered I can put my present obligations ahead of my emotions, for the good of my family. Why can't you do the same?"

"I'm trying, honey. A man deals with pain in a different way. Until I get to the bottom of who caused her death, I can't let it lie."

"It's been two years, Dillon. If there're no answers, are you putting your life on hold forever?"

"I'm not putting my life on hold, Janet." He said it with a little more venom than intended.

"I'm setting it as a priority, along with the other obligations a father and husband has."

She dropped her chin and eyed him with raised eyebrows. "We always seem to make this issue a difference of opinion, instead of something we should be unified on. We appear to be fighting two different wars on the same ground. You shut me out when you brood like this."

O'Malley felt bad. He knew he had to find a better way of dealing with his anger and grief. Hours of counseling by the FBI psychologists had not helped to ease the pain he felt for his daughter. His initial inclination to leave law enforcement would never have worked, as the period of stress leave merely provided more opportunity, for dwelling on the situation. After their loss, he begged to be allowed to return to normal duties much earlier than the FBI thought plausible.

"I'm sorry you feel that way. Perhaps we should leave the conversation for another time," he said.

Janet teared up, slammed the cutlery on the table, and stormed to the bedroom. The door banged shut before he could respond. He sat in stony silence and finished his meal. This is how any conversation about the loss of their daughter usually ended—an angry standoff. He knew she would cool down if he left her alone. It always took time and both of them understood that no answers existed to the questions, in their minds. Nothing would bring Fallon back to them.

In the morning, O'Malley went straight to his office at FBI headquarters. His anticipation of the Institute's attitude, with regard to use of the memory sweep, for crime resolution, had proved correct. Now he would need to convince his superior, Deputy Director Hadley, of the need to pursue the matter with one of the Supreme Court Judges. He needed to juggle his caseloads a little, in order to pursue the potential assassination plot. Hadley would want it that way, despite the fact he found no agreement with the president's policies. O'-Malley could not think of one person in his cir cle of friends and work colleagues, who supported America's new leader.

President Lewis came to power through the large number of blue-collard workers who felt disenfranchised through the many years of political greed and bungled foreign policies, which brought America into its current state of near bankruptcy. Lewis, a former high-profile business man, promised the middle class he would make America great once again.

He promised to bring jobs back to the country and strengthen the military in the fight against terrorism, but to date, no positive signs of these promises could be seen. The President's two saving graces hung on the fact that illegal immigration was down and Americans did not have to fear having their guns taken away. The rest of the President's campaign promises, however, appeared to have been empty posturing.

O'Malley's list of cases numbered forty-seven. In order of priority, they ranged from money laundering to businesses with links to organized crime and politicians who evaded taxes.

The assassination plot, although only a threat, ranked at the top of the list now.

"Did you go to the Institute?" He looked up at the office entrance where his boss, Deputy Director Hadley, leaned against the doorjamb.

"Yeah, it went as I expected," said O'Malley.

"Do you think it will be worth the sweat to get an injunction?"

"I do, but we have to hurry. Gracie Beauchamp is sinking. I doubt whether she will last another two days."

Hadley coughed and sat in a chair opposite O'Malley. He pulled out a small container from his breast pocket, removed a tiny tablet and place it under his tongue. "I'm not doing this for that bastard, Lewis. I couldn't give a rat's ass if someone took him out. This is for those two young sisters," said Hadley.

"I'm with you one hundred percent, Chief. It is, however, our civic duty to find the perpetrators of the supposed plot. Getting Prof

Wheeler to perform his magic can serve both ends."

Hadley grimaced. "You're right, of course. If there is a plot you can bet there are high rollers involved and that's dangerous for a democracy."

"You have a judge in mind, Chief?"

"I have a good rapport with Judge Stein-beck. I'll call him right away."

"I'm off to the hospital to check on Gracie. Call me when you have the injunction. I'll enjoy telling that hippy professor to hand over the keys," said O'Malley.

He left the building and walked to the car garage. The chrome on the black SUV glinted in the rays of the overhead, neon lighting as he approached the vehicle. He always enjoyed the raw power of the Chevy. Before turning the ignition, he sat in the driver's seat for a moment and glanced over the dash. A sudden thought came to him and he dialed his cell phone.

His wife answered.

"Hi, babe—got a moment?"

"If it's about last night, forget it. Nothing is going to change," she said.

"I just wanted to say I'm sorry. I never meant to shut you out—I love you, sweetheart."

"I know you don't mean to do it, Dillon, but I feel so alone. You won't even talk about what happened."

"I know, honey—it's my fault. I guess I've just never found a way to deal with it."

"It's hurting both of us."

"I know."

"Then do something about it before our marriage and our son become casualties."

"I will, honey—I promise. How's your day been so far, otherwise?"

"It's quiet, but Steven will be home from school soon. How's your day going?"

"All is well—just off to the hospital to check up on an assault victim. I'll be a little late. Don has me working on a priority case."

"Do you want me to keep dinner for you?"

"Sure. I'll see you later. Love you."

"Love you, too. Bye."

Janet's voice carried her resignation to the fate of being an agent's spouse. It went much deeper than the job, however. The loss of Fallon at the tender age of sixteen years in a drunk-driver episode raised a barrier, which seemed impossible to breach. To make matters worse, the drunk driver disappeared from the scene before the arrival of the police. They both knew their son, Steven, now in his fourteenth year, remained the one strong connector of the family. Life continued, with Dillon throwing himself into crime resolution and Janet into her Lady's Group at the church.

O'Malley started the Chevy and roared out of the garage into the street. Several minutes later, he arrived at the hospital, and parked in the restricted zone, allocated to law enforcement. He caught the elevator to the third-floor ward, where Gracie Beauchamp lay, strung up to a dozen tubes and two monitors. The guard recognized him and gave a casual nod.

Gracie's expressionless face exuded the pallor of death and the assisted-breathing apparatus worked the airflow in and out of her lungs on a rhythmical cycle. But for the sound of the equipment, all seemed perfectly peaceful. He hovered near her head and peered down at the closed eyelids for several moments, before taking the lone chair in the corner. His thoughts ranged from empathy to anger as he leaned forward to whisper words he knew she couldn't hear.

"I'll do my best to get to the bottom of this matter. I promise you."

The pain of his own loss surged, and he felt as though he was losing Fallon all over again.

The nurse on duty popped her head in the door. "She needs all the help she can get. You're FBI, aren't you?"

O'Malley looked up in surprise. "Yes, Special Agent O'Malley. Do you have any news regarding her condition?"

"It's not good I'm afraid, but she's a fighter. We can only wait and see. The lieutenant from the local precinct was also around to check on her this morning."

"Lieutenant Dunmore?" asked O'Malley.

"That's him. I hope you guys find her assailant and afford her a bit of justice."

"We will. I can promise you that."

The nurse smiled at him and left.

*

Assistant Director Hadley decided to pay Judge Steinbeck a personal visit and not discuss the matter of an injunction over the phone. He timed it well and found the judge in his chambers, on a court recess.

The judge looked up from his desk as Hadley knocked, opened the door, and peeked into the room. "Hi, Marvin."

"Don, please come in. How've you been lately?"

"I've been better. It hasn't been the same since that mild heart attack," said Hadley.

"You really need to look after yourself. Why don't you retire?"

"I will, next year. The wife and I have it all planned."

"That's great. Now, to what do I owe the pleasure of a visit from the FBI?"

The deputy director sat opposite Steinbeck.

"I need a favor." Hadley explained the position. He didn't get into specifics of names, but mentioned the potential of a presidential assassination and stressed the need to discover the villains before the evil deed could be accomplished.

"This could end up being a controversial decision," said the judge. "You're asking me to grant a preliminary injunction to force this institute into compliance, thereby gaining access to cutting edge technology. This could change the landscape of criminal investigation."

"I understand the implications, but if we don't use all the means at our disposal, and the President of the United States is taken out, the ramifications could be just as dire," said Hadley.

The judge considered the matter for a moment. "I read about the breakthrough in the Science Monitor. It does mean the Memory Intrusion Sweep has been advertised as a potential asset to mankind. This, however, doesn't condone the use of it for the purpose of criminal investigation—it will raise a similar debate we had to deal with in the Apple dilemma."

"The professor involved agreed to one thing: the sweep needed to undergo a test with a human target mind. This would afford them such an opportunity."

The judge felt conflicted. "A prelim injunction should be to restrain someone from using a potentially dangerous concept, not to force them to use it."

Hadley was not going to give up. "My point is, the breakthrough is going to be used or discarded, as a benefit to humankind. This injunction will achieve focus on a real life situation and possibly resolve a conspiracy at the same time."

"What about the target mind? I believe she's on death's door. What if the procedure kills her?"

Hadley considered the implication. "It's unlikely. According to the Institute's professor, more harm could come to the investigator than the target. If she did die, it would be more because of a broken neck—this intervention may save the President's life, plus catch her killer."

After another ten minutes of debate the judge gave in. "Okay, I'll grant you the injunction, but only after I've spoken to the dean of the Institute—I'll need to confirm certain ramifications of the breakthrough's use. I'll let you know my verdict in two, maybe three, hours."

Hadley thanked the judge and left.

*

O'Malley's secretary looked into the office and caught his attention. He glanced at his watch—6:15 p.m. "I'm heading home now, Dillon."

"Thanks for bringing the case progress status up to date," he said.

"You're welcome. See you tomorrow."

Hadley still hadn't called to let him know about the injunction. He thought of Gracie and wondered how much longer she could hold on. His cellphone jangled out the Star Spangled Banner and he snatched it up. "O'Malley."

He recognized the voice of the caller. "Special Agent? It's Professor Wheeler here, from the Institute of Neuro-Technology."

"Hello, Dr. Wheeler. What can I do for you?"

"Our dean has just shared the news of the injunction. Your assistant director apparently got a judge to agree."

"That's good news for me, and I guess bad news for you, Professor."

"Not particularly bad news. I've been talking it over with my colleague, Miss Pink, and we feel it may be a good thing."

"I'm glad you're coming onboard with the idea, Professor."

"It was more my colleague than I, Special Agent. She visited the victim at the hospital, hoping to get some idea about the patient's condition. While I, personally am not persuaded by the emotion of the moment, Miss Pink was very moved."

"So, we don't really need the injunction?" asked O'Malley.

"I prefer to have it because it gets the Institute off the hook for any libelous actions."

"I understand. I would like to know more about the process. We need to meet very soon and make an action plan. The victim is only just hanging on."

"That's why I've called," said Wheeler.

A noise at the door caused O'Malley to look up. The assistant director stood there, waiting for the call to end. "Are you free this evening, Dr. Wheeler? I can be there in about half an hour," asked O'Malley.

"I would prefer you to meet me at my home. My assistant, Miss Pink, will be here as well."

"Give me the address," said O'Malley. He wrote down the details on his desk calendar pad.With the call concluded Hadley spoke. "Sorry, I didn't get back to you straight away, Dillon. I got a call from a senator and it held me up. I see the dean has contacted you regarding the injunction."

"Actually, it was Professor Wheeler, and there seems to have been a change of heart. Apparently his assistant went to the hospital to see Gracie Beauchamp and it convinced her to cooperate."

Hadley pulled a handkerchief from his pocket and blew his nose. "The injunction will protect them. I can understand the professor's concerns."

"I'd better phone my wife and let her know I'll be later than anticipated," said O'Malley.

"Keep me abreast of things, Dillon. Don't go off half-cocked and cause any trouble."

O'Malley grinned. "As if I would do anything like that."

Don Hadley left and O'Malley reached for his cell again. "Hi, sweetheart—something's come up, and I'll be a bit later than I thought. I'll grab a quick bite at the diner."

∞∞

4

Earlier that Day

"I'm being absolutely serious, Mr. President."

"Are you sure someone isn't playing a joke," said the President.

"No, sir. The intel comes from the CIA and I stress—we do not know how serious a threat it is, however, you should take no chances."

"Do you think it's the Russians?"

"We have no leads other than a woman, who was told this information on a one-night stand and died as a consequence of it. The woman's sister, who apparently found the diary was also attacked and left for dead. Unfortunately, she's in a coma and is unlikely to wake up."

"No foreign connections?"

"Not that we know of, Mr. President."

Martin Lewis stared out of the oval office window. "That doesn't mean it's not the Russians, or that silly little bastard in North Korea."

"We can't rule out anyone at this stage, Mr. President. It could even be the opposition. You haven't made any friends in the senate or the house."

"Don't blame me for others not wanting to go along with my policies. I know I'm unpopular."

"I'm just saying, Sir." The chief of staff looked at his shoes with embarrassment. "I know what you're saying, John, but I don't have to like it."

"I understand, Sir."

"Get the hell out of here and leave me alone for a while. I need to think."

The chief of staff obeyed the blunt order with enthusiasm. The president made life difficult for all his staff. No appreciation for loyalty or service ever escaped his lips and no staff member in the entire White House enjoyed being in his presence. His foreign policies had countries in the trenches and the chief couldn't think of a worse president since Carter. His job, however, required loyalty and he made it a daily practice to tell himself he did it for the country he loved. No wonder someone wanted to assassinate the man.

*

Martin Lewis sat at the desk, which had served many presidents over the years and scowled. People were so fickle. Most of his staff didn't have an intelligent bone between their ears and he often felt like firing the lot of them. He longed for the days when his businesses provided him with all the personal esteem and financial security he needed. To run for office although a prestigious endeavor, seemed a natural progression of status for him and it added power to his position in life—the kind of power one couldn't garner in business. He never gave the problems and headaches, which came with the office any thought, until the day he moved in. Lewis keyed the intercom to open the line to his secretary. "Tell my service detail I wish to make my usual visit."

"Right away, Mr. President."

Lewis walked out the side entrance of the office and traipsed down the long hallway to the secure exit, which led to the presidential garage. His detail of secret service agents waited to take him to a place in the city he often visited. The rumor had it he met with an old and wise counsellor, a friend from way back in his business days, but the President's real motives were not known. If the security detail knew, they wouldn't say, and they wouldn't pry. No one could take a chance with him. He held too much power and paid a lot of money out in bonuses and favors for those who did his bidding.

The secret service agent opened the door of the presidential SUV and Lewis felt himself dissolve into the soft leather seat. They knew exactly where he wanted to go and as the vehicle pulled out, two other SUVs followed with another in front of the procession. The detail made a turn into an alley and stopped at the back of an old apartment complex.

The security men went about their task of checking all possible hiding places before the driver opened the door for the president to step out. One agent followed behind him as he walked brusquely to an entrance in the rear of the complex.

Another agent dodged ahead, opened the door and scurried up the narrow steps, to the first floor. He nodded the all clear and the president made for a door in the hallway. He opened it and stopped to look back at the men and gave them a knowing look. They took up positions outside and kept watch.

"Hello, my sweetheart."

"I've been waiting for hours, Martin," the woman said.

Her long blonde hair flowed over straight, bony shoulders and cascaded down her back. At thirty-one, she retained attractiveness and the freshness of a young girl, beautiful and elegant. That's how Martin Lewis liked his women. There were several of them and whenever he wanted to whet his appetite, one was always available. A well-kept secret.

They embraced and she kissed him hungrily. He couldn't wait and carted her off to the bedroom where they divested themselves of their clothing and fell into one another's arms.

An hour later, he kissed the girl one more time and got dressed.

She sat on the bed and looked at him. "Are you stressed, Martin?"

"In case you haven't noticed, I have a stressful job."

"I know, my love, but today you seemed a little distant."

"Someone wants me dead. The FBI has picked up on a lead which indicates someone is planning my assassination."

"Oh, Martin, honey. I'm so sorry. I didn't mean to pry, but that's awful."

"Yeah. Someone is sitting in a living room somewhere making a plan to ambush me and it doesn't feel good."

She got off the bed and came to him. "Come here, darling. Let me ease your mind a little."

He smiled at her naivety. "You don't really have a clue, do you?"

She looked at him pensively. "What would you have me do?"

"Just drop it. I shouldn't have told you."

She became all tearful and buried her head in his chest.

"I have to go, sweetheart. I'll see you soon. Wait for my call."

She nodded and unwrapped her arms from around his neck. Lewis turned and walked to the door. "Don't read too much into it," he said.

The security detail jumped into action the moment Lewis exited the apartment and took up defensive positions around him. The President double-timed down the stairs to the building's back door and jumped into the back of the presidential vehicle while the agents scurried to their vehicles, their heads swiveling in all directions, pistols at the ready.

"Back to the White House," he shouted. The SUV shot down the alley to the opposite end and broadsided into the main street. Ten minutes later, the entourage arrived at the secure entrance and Lewis disembarked. Back in the White House suite, his wife, Sheila, looked up in surprise. "Back so soon?"

"Where are my cigars? Pour me a drink."

She dutifully went to the liquor cabinet and poured a tot of bourbon for him. She stretched on her toes to reach a box of cigars which lay open on the top shelf of the cabinet.

"Here you are, darling. Why the worried look?"

"The CIA says someone is out to get me. They're looking into the matter."

Sheila, about to light the cigar for him stopped. "Oh my god, Martin. Are you serious?"

"Of course, I'm serious, woman," he groused.

"You don't have to be so angry."

"Sorry, love. I'm a little wound up at the moment."

She moved closer and placed her arms around his waist. "Don't worry, sweetheart. The FBI will find out who it is and deal with it."

Sheila Lewis, in her mid-forties, still retained a slim figure and loved to dress like a fashion model. Her support for her husband's unpopular stance in politics did not waiver, despite all the negative comments made by his critics and the press. Her commitment, however, came at a price. She suspected her husband's infidelity.

*

Special Agent O'Malley made his way to Port Morris, a light industrial area with warehouse., He wondered why Professor Wheeler would want to live in the area. Two features, closeness to the waterfront and a view of the islands, most likely tempted some people to turn an old industrial building into a home, but it would not suit his tastes. Janet would hate it, too far from schools and shops.

He found the address and parked the Chevy outside the main roll-up door in the front of the double-story building. Next to a single metal door, beside the roll-up which appeared to be the entrance to the upper level, stood a scooter on its stand. In the absence of a bell to ring, O'Malley knocked as loudly as he could and waited. An electric lock clicked and the door jumped an inch inward. A voice shouted, "Come in, Special Agent."

A flight of stairs faced him, and without hesitation, O'Malley climbed to the top where the professor waited on the landing. "Please, step into my humble abode, Special Agent O'-Malley."

The landing opened into a cavernous room, filled with modern furniture and space-age light fixtures. Raw, red brick gave the room an effect of an old fire station and the sea-facing wall sported a huge bay window, which revealed a panoramic view of the North and South Brother islands. O'Malley, captivated by the scene, walked to the window and stared with amazement at the vista.

Samantha Pink's voice arrested him and he turned to see the funky neurophysicist standing behind a counter, which acted as a divider between the kitchen and the main living area. "It's a great view, isn't it?"

O'Malley smiled. "Fascinating. I wondered why anybody would want to live out here, but now I can see a good reason."

Samantha's sparkly blue eyes contained a hint of humor as she creased her lips into a wide smile to display a stark contrast between her pearly white teeth and dark purple lipstick. The trendy, pink colored hair suited her and the curvy hips drew his eyes like a magnet. When O'Malley first saw her at the institute she wore a white, lab coat which did not reveal much of her figure but now, despite the funkiness, he saw her as an attractive woman.

"Can I offer you something to drink, Special Agent?"

"Please call me Dillon—No thanks, I'm still on duty. Do you have something non-alcoholic?"

She turned to open the fridge and came out with a club soda. "Will soda and lime juice do?"

"Just fine, thanks."

She poured the drink and handed it to him. "Luke?"

"I'll have a beer, Sam, thank you."

O'Malley took a sip and then his inquisitive side showed up. "Forgive me for asking, but are you two—" He hesitated in embarrassment and the professor quickly jumped in.

"We're good friends, close work colleagues, but just good friends."

Samantha rolled her eyes and said nothing. The action conveyed a brief expression of apparent frustration and was not lost on the agent.

He concluded there had to be more to the relationship than met the eye.

Lucas gestured toward one of the chairs and O'Malley sat on the sofa. Samantha sat next to him and moved uncomfortably close, all the while eyeing him with an intense contemplation. He placed his hands, palms down on his knees, to purposely show off his wedding ring. She kept him under scrutiny and seemed un

deterred by his obvious discomfort, while sipping at her drink.

"I want to clarify my position regarding the use of the memory sweeper," said Lucas.

O'Malley gave a brief smile and waited for the professor to elaborate.

"I am not specifically against the use of the concept to fight crime. In fact, I believe it could revolutionize investigations. The consequences, however, might prove more of a problem for law enforcement than expected."

"I appreciate where you're coming from, Professor, but I believe it should be for law enforcement and government to decide. In the meantime, we have a unique opportunity to test the waters and do something good for innocent people."

"I understand that, but we are going to invade someone else's mind without their consent. We are going to have access to all the private thoughts and inclinations of this young woman, and I am conflicted as to the violation of her private life, versus the possible knowledge we gain of the killer."

Sam jumped in. "Oh for God's sake, Luke. Do you honestly think she'll care about her private thoughts in the face of preventing a possible assassination and the discovery of her killer?"

"If she lives, she may take umbrage at the notion that her private thoughts were paraded before someone else's eyes," countered Lucas.

O'Malley could see the argument might escalate, unless he intervened. He put up his hand. "I appreciate you both have differing opinions about the matter but the fact is, we have an injunction, to perform the experiment. We should be discussing how this is going to work and leave our sentiments out of it."

Lucas narrowed his eyelids. "It's fine for you,

Dillon. But we have the Institute's reputation to think of. Despite the injunction, our names will also be dragged through the news—possibly in a negative fashion."

"You'll have to rationalize the concept in your conscience, Professor. Whatever way you look at it, the injunction forces the Institute to comply. There isn't much you can really do about it."

Samantha interrupted. "Lucas is just a being a wet blanket. He is actually excited about seeing how the sweep works."

"I may be a wet blanket but you're a loose cannon without a scope," said Lucas.

O'Malley wanted to know more about how the process worked. "Whoa, let's back up here a little and bring some order to the meeting."

Samantha glared at Lucas, who grinned like the Cheshire Cat. The special agent looked from one to the other and said, "Please can we try to be nice to each other?"

∞∞

5

Three Days Previous

Bob watched from a safe distance. The un-marked Ford, parked in front of Gracie Beauchamp's apartment block, belonged to the New York City Police. As expected via the call he intercepted, between Gracie and the local precinct, Lieutenant Dunmore arrived on time to pick up Veronica's diary. Bob couldn't see the door of the apartment from his vantage point, but he wanted to see what further action the police might take. Several minutes later, he heard the sirens. An ambulance appeared at the end of the street and raced to screech to a halt in front of the apartment.

Bob froze. Gracie surely could not still be alive? His worst fears came to fruition as the paramedics, after disappearing into the build-ing came out again, carefully pushing a gurney with a body strapped on it. This could only mean one thing: he'd slipped up.

The ambulance raced off with sirens blaring and he decided to follow. At the hospital, the paramedics removed the gurney with its passenger and entered the emergency entrance. Bob parked in the lot and walked through the ER doors to see a hive of activity as nurses ran to and fro from the reception to the operating theaters. A doctor flashed past him in a hurry and the intercom blared for assistance for the latest inductee.

He took a seat outside one of the consulting rooms and waited. The police lieutenant arrived and shortly after, a uniformed cop; both waited outside the operating theatre. Bob chided himself for not making sure his victim was dead. Before Veronica, the last time he killed anyone had been in Afghanistan, a skirmish with members of the Taliban. Now in the space of two weeks, he had killed two people, well, one definite and one potential. He didn't feel good about it.

He thought of the past and how he came to be in the present predicament. The deterioration of his circumstances began in the final days of the U.S. presence in Afghanistan, when a ground operation, which should have been a walk in the park, turned into a disaster in the aftermath of his order to open fire. Unfortunately for him, the contingent in hiding amongst the derelict and burned-out chassis of some civilian buses turned out to be an allied force. They were part of a Canadian coalition backup, seeking the same enemy.

The full instructions, ignored by Bob at the time, called for him not to open fire until verification of identity. He should have known about the Canadians. Twenty-three men died because of him. To carry this emotional load already constituted a sentence for him, but the fact he managed to hide his miscalculation and have the consequent investigation reduced to a "friendly-fire" incident, amounted to a more heinous crime. Only one other person knew the truth, but the testimony would never be heard at the enquiry.

In what one might term as a huge, providential stroke of luck for Bob, a junior officer under his command had been caught red-handed in the rape of a local girl, days prior to the fire fight. The girl's parents approached Bob with photographic evidence of the crime and he paid them off in order to save the military's reputation from being tarnished.

As a commander of an incursion unit, the intention had been to discipline his junior officer, however, when the friendly-fire incident took place with the same officer as the only witness to his crime, Bob decided to use the indiscretion to his advantage. Nothing with regard to his own bad decision would ever be known, and in exchange, he would remain silent about the junior officer's crime.

Whoever sent him the blackmail letters had full access to all military records, but he couldn't even begin to fathom how his situation came to be known, or the identity of his blackmailer. Unless he obeyed the instructions, his future looked bleak and there would be no pension for him in his old age. The military tribunal overseeing the incident exonerat

ed him of blame based on the testimony of his junior officer, who stated their radio-communications were disrupted at the time, and the coalition force had fired on them first, giving no option but to return the fire. Several months later the junior officer died in an a mysterious accident.

At the end of his deployment, Bob managed to get a position with the Secret Service, a job he enjoyed and did not want to lose. The blackmail letters came as a nasty surprise and threw his life into turmoil. The evening at the nightclub, which involved young Veronica and his unfortunate admission of an involvement in a presidential assassination attempt, constituted his worst mistake. It had been a moment of weakness which followed a week of the most severe depression he had ever known.

*

Lucas and Samantha eyed each other out for a moment and then acquiesced to O'Malley's interjection for restraint.

"I need you to explain to me, in brief layman's terms, how the process works. Let's leave the morality of the issue out of it for the moment. What exactly is the memory sweeper?"

Again, Lucas and Samantha ogled each other to see who would be better at an explanation in more simplified terms.

"You go ahead, Luke. You're the professor," said Samantha.

Lucas grinned. "Oh, yeah? It was originally your idea, until you needed an intelligent mind to make some sense of it."

Samantha pulled a face and stuck out her tongue. O'Malley sensed his frustrations rising again and said, "I'm sure either of you are absolutely capable of giving me the lowdown. But let's get serious here for a second. I understand this to be the breakthrough of the century, but for a real test of its effectiveness, this could win both of you a Nobel Prize."

"He wouldn't know what to do with such a prize, but I could certainly use the money," said Samantha.

O'Malley looked up at the ceiling in despair before Lucas came to the rescue.

"Okay, all jokes aside. The memory sweeper is a device that can take the mind of an inves-

tigator and transport it into the mind of someone else—the target mind. We have found a
way to absorb a part of an investigator's mind
into an avatar, which is transported into the
target's mind by the use of a particle accelerator. The process is under the instruction of an
extremely sophisticated computer program."

"What do you use as an avatar?" asked O'-
Malley.

"The avatar is a grouping of information-
bearing particles capable of assimilating the
conscious mind of the investigator, extracting
it from the right side of the brain and transporting it via a specially designed conduit, to
the target's memory banks."

"Why the right side of the brain?"

Samantha jumped in to give an explanation. "The content of every thought you devel-
op is built into a double memory concept and
is

staged in each brain's hemisphere. The
right hemisphere builds the concept from the
larger picture to smaller detail. The left revers-

es that procedure—we use the right side because we want the detail."

Lucas continued. "There is a quantum-entangled effect between the particles of each hemisphere, which maintain an immediate contact with each other. This contact does not diminish while the right-sided consciousness of the investigator is invading the target's memory banks."

O'Malley looked thoughtful. "So consciousness continues for the investigator, from a left brain point of view, despite the fact that the right brain duplication is invading the target's brain—the total thought process is in two states at one time."

"I see you understand a bit about quantum mechanics, Special Agent."

"Please, call me Dillon," said O'Malley.

Without any encouragement, Samantha continued the explanation. "The computer software program is in contact with the grouping of particles and is also able to record the investigator's thoughts. The investigators commentary and thoughts are stored in a computer file, thereby allowing the investigator access to things witnessed within the memory banks of the target, afterward."

"What exactly will the investigator witness during the tour, and how?" asked O'Malley.

"The investigator, we think, will see the scenes in a holographic form. This has never been done before, so we're not sure but theoretically the investigator's right brain consciousness will be inside the scenarios stored within whatever memory is being witnessed," answered Lucas.

"This is extraordinary," said O'Malley. "So, the scenes will be recorded in a similar form—you would be able to play them back like a movie?"

"We believe so—but again, I must caution; we'll only know for sure after the initial experiment is concluded," said Samantha.

O'Malley stared out the window for a few moments before his next question. "Does the investigator have any contact with the outside world while this is going on?"

Lucas looked at Samantha, who nodded. "The only contact with the outside world will be in the form of an awareness of the room, in which the sweep is taking place. This awareness will provide an indirect connection, only. The avatar, which consists of the investigator's right brain consciousness in conjunction with the grouping of particles, and the computer program whom we have named Echo, will be projected into the target's memory. Samantha insisted that Echo be a feminine touch and will govern the function of the entire process—essentially Echo is just a name with a personality she has given to the software."

"I trust Echo is as charming and bright as you are, Samantha," said O'Malley.

Samantha reddened visibly at O'Malley's words.

"Oh, Echo's just like her creator: fruity and unpredictable," said Lucas.

"She's not—you're such an idiot, sometimes, Lucas Wheeler."

"Lame-brain," said Lucas. She grabbed a magazine from under the side table, and threw it at him.

O'Malley shut his eyes and bowed his head. He wondered what sort of progress he would make if the future held this type of open warfare. Wheeler and Pink obviously respected each other's professional acumen. Despite the noisy, derogatory banter, their relationship appeared to have a closeness, which allowed them to malign each other with absurdities. He couldn't figure out if the mock hostility represented familiarity or something else, perhaps love. If they were in love with each other, they certainly had a strange way of showing it.

Lucas picked up the magazine and moved back to his seat. "Echo is a wonderful guide, and she knows more about neuroscience than the two of us put together. The dean, through his high-end contacts, made sure she would have full access to the Neuro Federation's vast resources and databases. There is no neurological disorder, malady, or anything in the world of neuroscience she couldn't diagnose or suggest a remedy for."

"What about the dangers? You indicated earlier on, there could be a danger to the investigator."

Lucas squinted at O'Malley. "Things can happen. We can only guess at some of the brain functions which might upset the avatar on its unfamiliar journey. The glial cells pose perhaps the greatest threat. These cells are the pruners of the vine, so to speak, and trim away weaker memories. There are trillions of neurons to be cleaned and serviced by these cells, which means twice as many glials than neurons. It's possible the avatar will be detected by the brain as a threat and the glial cells will attack in an effort to stave off possible dangerous effects."

"The worst possible scenario is that the avatar is disrupted or destroyed in the process of such an attack, which means the investigator will lose that part of the conscious plurality. We have no idea what would happen in such a case, should the mind in the left brain and retained within the investigator's head, be the only part that remains," said Samantha.

Lucas added, "It would simply mean having to think with half one's mind—you do that all the time, Sam."

Samantha's face took on a good impression of an approaching thunderstorm. "Lucas!"

O'Malley decided he had heard enough and stood. "I must get going. I assume we'll need to move the patient to the lab at the institute?"

"Yes, it would be difficult to move the accelerator and all the apparatus to the hospital. I will arrange a space close to the induction harness, so a bed can be brought in. You'll need to arrange everything with the dean. There isn't a great deal of space so any medical staff the hospital supplies will need to stand outside in the hallway," said Lucas.

"We'll have to hurry as the target brain is ailing. Will her poor condition affect the experiment?"

"As long as she's alive and the brain's still working, the memory banks should be accessible," said Samantha.

"I have one more request," said O'Malley.

Lucas and Samantha stood in unison and waited.

"I want to be the investigator."

The scientists both rounded on him. "Absolutely not."

O'Malley inclined his head and frowned. "Why not?"

Lucas cleared his throat and Samantha moved uncomfortably close to O'Malley to stare into his eyes in an intimidating way. "There is a language and a protocol only we know, which is in use with the software and the avatar. It would take too long to train you."

O'Malley felt a little deflated. "I see. Well, I guess you're it, then," he said.

"Besides, either Sam or I should be the first to use the device we designed and built."

"You're right, Professor. Hopefully the record will work in a way that I can view it afterward. I know what we're looking for, and it may be in hidden facts a non-law enforcer would not recognize."

"So, I guess this will all happen on the morrow? Sam and I will need to spend time setting up the system for the experiment."

"I will contact the dean tonight, and we'll proceed first thing in the morning," said O'-Malley.

Sam drew even closer to the special agent and before he could back off she placed her arms around him and kissed him affectionately on the cheek. "Take care, Dillon. I've always wanted to do that to an FBI guy."

O'Malley went red in the face but smiled obligingly. "You shouldn't say that, Sam. You'll have all the guys in my department lining up and there are a couple thousand."

She grinned. "Bring em on, sweetie."

O'Malley looked at Lucas who raised his eyebrows. "Is she always like this, Professor?"

"She's one of a kind, Dillon—no one can figure her out."

They walked down the stairs to the entrance, and O'Malley headed for the Chevy.

He opened the door and turned. "Until tomorrow, then?"

"See you in the morning. Thanks for coming by," said Lucas.

"Stay cute, Mister FBI man," said Samantha.

∞∞

6

The Memory Sweep

After O'Malley's visit to the hospital, Bob knew something needed to be done before Gracie Beauchamp regained consciousness. A second guard posted outside the ward complicated his plan to gain entry and finish the job. On his second visit, enquiries made of a junior nurse, confirmed Gracie's condition to be deteriorating. Either way he needed to make sure. What he did glean regarding her future, however, caused him some concern.

The young nurse mentioned that Gracie was to be moved to another clinic for specialized treatment the following morning. Bob didn't take any chances and returned at 4:00 a.m. to wait. At 6:30, an ambulance pulled up outside the hospital and he knew it had to be for Gracie Beauchamp. He followed at a distance, and eventually, the vehicle pulled into the grounds of the Neuro-Technical Institute.

Bob parked his truck outside the gates and pulled out his phone. He did a quick search on the Internet and came up with an article regarding the institute's latest breakthrough regarding memory intrusion. In an instant he knew what the FBI wanted to do. He needed to prepare himself. If they managed to pull it off, Gracie's memory might give vital details away, which could lead them to his identity. He pulled into the early morning traffic with urgency and drove aggressively back to his apartment.

*

O'Malley greeted the dean with cordiality. "Is everything set up and ready?"

"The professor and Samantha are testing the particle circuit. It will take another ten minutes or so," answered the dean.

"What is it with this couple?" asked O'Malley.

"Don't judge the book by the cover, Special Agent. I know they come across as quirky and strange, but their combined synergy and knowledge has put us on the forefront of neuroscience. Despite the obvious eccentricities, they are both delightfully invigorating souls."

"I struggle to work out what their real feelings for one another are," said O'Malley.

"I believe it's an enigma to everyone who works here, the students included. I doubt whether they know themselves."

O'Malley grinned. "I guess it makes life more interesting for everyone. I can't wait to see if the experiment is successful. I know you folk are a little conflicted as to the application, but I only see the greater good being served through all this."

"It is what it is, Special Agent. I am glad the decision is out of our hands, though. Here comes the professor."

Lucas bounded toward them with vigor. "Greetings, Dillon," he said. "We are almost ready to begin the experiment. There is just one more detail." He produced a piece of paper which contained a typewritten paragraph.

"What's this, Professor," asked O'Malley.

"It simply states that the FBI takes full responsibility for the outcome of the experiment."

O'Malley laughed. "It's an unnecessary step, Professor. The judge who granted the injunction takes the blame if anything goes wrong."

Lucas looked a little deflated. "Oh, well, yes, of course—I guess you're right. I'm just making extra sure."

"Don't worry about your reputation. This experiment will only show the Institute's willingness to help catch Veronica Beauchamp's killer and hopefully circumvent an assassination," said O'Malley.

"I gotcha," said Lucas.

Two tough looking agents sidled up to them, each with an automatic weapon in hand

and addressed O'Malley. "Where do want us to position ourselves, sir?"

"There is limited space in the lab—you guys should be right outside the door. After the experiment begins no one is allowed in."

The two men nodded and took up positions on each side of the lab entrance. A doctor from the hospital, whom the FBI had vetted the day before, came out of the lab. "The patient is hooked up to the apparatus. She is extremely frail, so I suggest you get on with the process. If the heart monitor should flatline, I'll come in and see if there's anything that can be done."

O'Malley thanked the doctor, who took a seat on a chair in the hallway. He turned to Lucas. "Are we ready?"

Lucas closed his eyes for a moment and said, "I'm ready to do the investigation. Let's go in."

He turned and walked through into the lab with O'Malley in tow.

*

Bob unlocked the door to his apartment and hurried inside. He went straight to a living room cabinet and pulled open the bottom drawer. After taking out a box, he placed it on the cabinet top and removed the lid. He pulled out two small canisters and a 9 mm parabellum. Each canister contained a concentration of Kolokol-1, a gas used by Russian troops in a Chechen uprising. The gas caused incapacitation and unconsciousness within seconds if inhaled within a reasonably confined space, such as a room or hallway.

Bob's training in the secret service armed him with the knowledge and use of such agents. He didn't want to kill anyone unnecessarily and knew there might be a guard placed outside the area, probably a laboratory. The incapacitation of an outside guard would only take a few seconds to effect and give him time to kill Gracie. The second canister would be for any occupants inside the lab. The parabellum, not a weapon used in the secret service, would seal the deal and he could make good his escape.

Satisfied with his small arsenal, Bob hurried back to his truck and pulled away with a screech of tires, to head to the Institute. The traffic slowed his progress and at times he swerved around vehicles to get ahead. A minute later the lights of a patrol car lit up his rearview mirror and a siren blared out its toxic message. Bob mumbled a profanity and pulled over to the curb, angry at himself for being so stupid. The patrol car parked behind him and he waited—the officer would be checking the registration. He pulled out his Secret Service badge and kept it handy with his driver's license. The cop exited his vehicle and walked up to the truck.

Bob rolled the window down and held out his badge with his license. The officer grabbed them for closer scrutiny. "In a hurry?"

"I'm working on a detail and I'm a bit late, Officer."

The officer nodded. "Okay, but be careful." He handed the badge and license back.

"Thanks, Officer. You have yourself a good day."

The cop turned and walked back to his vehicle without a second glance. Bob breathed a sigh of relief and pulled away again, a little more sedately. "The idiot just cost me valuable time," he muttered. When the traffic thinned a bit, he hit the gas pedal and glanced at the dash clock—forty minutes of elapsed time since he left the Institute.

Seven minutes later, he pulled up outside the gates of the Neuro Science Institute and clambered out of the truck. With the canisters and parabellum in the side pocket of his jacket, Bob moved stealthily through the gates and into the beautiful gardens which lined the driveway to the Institute's front entrance.

Several trees and bushes hid his approach. He spied a door at the side of the main building, which appeared to lead into a hallway and he took it, to move quietly toward its end. The hallway opened into a main foyer, where he looked up to see the signage, which indicated the whereabouts of the lab.

The foyer, deserted for the moment due to the early hour, revealed four other passages and he searched the signs to determine his destination. He crept down the relevant hallway with his revolver at the ready, in case of trouble.

The corridor took a sudden turn to the left and Bob approached the corner with care. He stopped to peer around the corner and saw two guards, each with automatic weapons. They stood on each side of door which he presumed to be the entrance to the lab. A man in a white coat, whom he presumed to be a doctor, sat on a chair against the opposite wall. The distance to the entrance appeared to be less than thirty feet.

*

O'Malley caught his first sight of the Memory Sweeper. Against the opposite wall stood a large box-like piece of equipment. Lucas started to explain some of the detail.

"That is the particle accelerator which contains the apparatus for shooting the information-bearing particles through this tube, in a continuous beam. Magnets are built in at intervals, along the distance of the tube, which accelerate the particles to a certain speed."

He pointed to another barrel-like object on the tube, about ten feet from the accelerator. "This is the particle diverter, which takes off a batch of the particles to form the avatar and the speed is adjusted to a snail's pace, for entry into the target brain."

Gracie Beauchamp lay on a gurney, strapped down, pale and gaunt—if O'Malley didn't know better, he would have sworn she was dead. A titanium harness embraced the top half of her cranium and a host of tiny red LED's blinked on and off, on an attached panel.

Samantha greeted him with a smile. "Welcome to the house of horrors," she said.

"I'm afraid it's a little over my head," said O'Malley.

"Don't worry, my pet. Aunty Sam will hold your hand through the whole ordeal."

O'Malley frowned at her. "I'm sure that won't be necessary, thank you. I'll just stand here, over to the side and observe."

"Suit yourself, honey. But I'm right here if you feel faint."

O'Malley cast Lucas and the dean a furtive glance and they both smiled. Lucas stepped up to a chair and sat, while Samantha pulled down a harness similar to the one on Gracie and attached it to the professor's head. A similar row of LEDs blinked on and off while she fussed around with a clamping process, which assured the harnesses position throughout the experiment. A thick cable ran from the harness to the particle tube which seemed to be the main transit avenue for the avatar to visit the professor's right brain hemisphere, from where his consciousness would be transported, into the system. Lucas appeared unfazed by the whole idea and O'Malley could only guess at what the professor's real thoughts were.

"Particle accelerator on." said Samantha. She stood at the keyboard of the master computer that ran the entire show. A buzzing and clicking sound emanated from the accelerator, as the power built up in the system.

"Particle beam initiated." she exclaimed. "All beam sensors are on and all is well."

Lights turned from red to green as the power surged and brought the beam of initiated particles in the tube to optimum, operation velocity. The dean stood behind her and peered over her shoulder at the screen, which reeled off numbers and a picture of the beam.

Samantha turned to O'Malley. "The internal cameras are showing the particle beam in section—you are not seeing the actual particles but the computer's assimilation. Once the beam is at velocity, we'll divert a grouping of particles to the harness on Lucas's head."

O'Malley stared at the screen. "What will actually happen to him, after the beam picks up his consciousness?"

"His left hemisphere will receive information from its counterpart and store the target brain's memories in his own memory bank. The right hemisphere, now caught up by the avatar, will see the target's memories and store them via the quantum entangled communication phenomenon into Lucas's memory, alongside the left hemisphere record."

"He will have two recollections of the same event?"

Samantha turned and eyed O'Malley. "I'm glad to see you're not just another pretty face, Dillon."

"But will Lucas be awake and lucid throughout the process?"

"In theory, yes—however, his left hemisphere will be focusing on the information being streamed to it from the avatar, so he will most likely appear to be asleep," said the dean.

They turned from the computer screen and looked at Lucas. He stared at them and said, "Well, what's everyone looking at—let's get on with it."

Samantha stuck her tongue out at him and made a face. "Stand by, initiating diversion."

She keyed in an instruction and the LEDs on the harness turned green. Lucas leaned back in the chair and closed his eyes.

∞∞

7

Spousal Confrontation.

Sheila Lewis enjoyed the attentions received from the other members of the fundraising function, one of several she had attended over the previous months. Apart from a few well-known faces of the local political wives club, most of the patrons appeared to be social neophytes and the spouses of rich donors. Their project focused on war veteran health care, and as main speaker for the event, Sheila's speech drew much positive acknowledgment. She sat at a table with several new donors, who couldn't take their eyes off her, all wanting to contribute to the cause and she languished in the attention. One woman in particular who happened to be sitting alongside Sheila, leaned over and started up a conversation.

"It must be difficult to be a first lady," she said.

"It has its downside, for sure," said Sheila.

"Your husband's a very busy man. I guess you don't get much time together," said the woman.

"Not as much as I would like."

The woman inclined her head. "My daughter lives in an apartment outside the main area of Manhattan and she's sure she saw the presidential's SUV park in an alley behind a building, onto which her bedroom window faces. She was so excited."

The first lady did her best not to react. "That's strange. I've never known him to park in back allies or secluded places. It would pose a security risk for them."

"My daughter recognized the vehicle and four others like it. She said the security agents all jumped out and checked the buildings and alley, before the president got out. Apparently, he zipped into a doorway and visited someone for at least two hours."

Sheila Lewis could not help the look of disdain on her face. "I don't meddle in my husband's official business."

"Of course not. I understand that. All I'm saying is it was a moment's excitement for my daughter," said the woman.

"Please excuse me," said the first lady. She stood and walked to the restroom, followed by her security detail, Agent Coulson, who took up a position outside the entrance.

In a cubicle, where prying eyes could not see, Sheila sat on the commode and cried. In her heart, she knew why her husband had been seen in a back alley. It was not the first time she received such a report, and in the past she tried to explain it away on something official, but the burgeoning truth frightened her—another woman.

She would confront him on the matter, but try to avoid a scene. Martin Lewis did not take accusations lightly and most likely he would have some sort of answer, which she could not prove to be wrong. His agents covered for him like they did for every other president. She disliked the attitude of the secret service—all of them, except her personal detail, Agent Coulson. He too, however, would be sworn to secrecy regarding the President's movements.

Sheila dried her eyes and exited the cubicle to wash her face. She needed to be alone for a while and made a decision to leave the function in her aide's capable hands.

"Agnes, please take over. I'm heading home. If anyone asks, tell them I'm feeling tired and render my apologies to the organizers."

"Yes, ma'am, don't worry about a thing. I'll take care of it," said the aide.

"Thanks, Agnes. You're a star."

She beckoned to Agent Coulson and indicated she would be leaving. He obediently followed and escorted her to the First Lady's SUV, outside, at the building's entrance. The driver jumped out and held the door open while Coulson and a second agent scrutinized the immediate surroundings. Coulson then jumped into the front passenger seat and the second agent headed for his own vehicle.

Back at home, Sheila went straight to the liquor cabinet and poured a martini. She never drank during the day, but the present situation warranted something to calm her. Outside on the back patio, she sat quietly sipping her drink. Agent Coulson appeared and stood in front of her. "Will you be requiring me to hang around, ma'am?"

"No, Agent Coulson. I could do with some alone time."

"I understand, ma'am. I'll be back in the morning for that trip to your daughter's school."

The first lady looked a bit blank and then suddenly remembered. "Oh yes, thank you, Agent. I'll see you in the morning."

Coulson left her to her thoughts.

Later that afternoon, the president wandered into the residence and made for the liquor cabinet. "Sheila? You home?" he shouted.

The first lady left her seat on the patio and joined her husband in the living room.

"Hi, honey. How's your day been so far?" she asked.

"Meetings and more meetings," he said.

"How about your meeting in that back alley in Manhattan the other day?"

The President frowned. "What do you mean?"

She relayed the story, told her by the woman at the fundraiser.

"She must be mistaken. It must have been one of the senators, or congress people."

"She recognized you, Martin."

"She has to be mistaking me for someone else," said the President.

"For god's sake, Martin—tell me the truth for once. Everyone knows what you look like."

"I can't divulge the nature of the business," he mumbled.

"You can't divulge its nature because we both know it wasn't official presidential business."

"You've got it wrong, Sheila. Just drop it," he said. His harsh tone indicated there would be no further discussion.

"You're seeing another woman, aren't you?"

"Drop it, Sheila." The president's face turned red.

She knew he was lying through his teeth.

*

Lucas heard a buzzing and a warm sensation seeped into his cerebral cortex as the beam of information-bearing particles invaded his mind. At the outset, when the memory sweep still existed as a concept, the moment of this present experience seemed an eternity from reality. And yet, here he sat in the chair, hooked up to the system, waiting for the first ever incursion into another person's memory.

It felt surreal. Despite his calm exterior, internalized emotions soared to heights never before experienced. A gamut of sensations overtook him, all at once—excitement, fear, elation, pride. They careened at him from every direction, and it took all his willpower to stave off a panic attack.

Vaguely, Samantha's voice filtered through to Lucas's consciousness but another sensation, made its presence known. A part of him started to lift and sway like a sail in a windstorm. His mind experienced a sudden forward motion and shaking, yet his body remained glued to the chair. A soft indigo hue surrounded the immediate area of perception and intuitively, Lucas understood it had not come by physical eyesight. A better term might have been the 'eyes of the soul,' or the 'insight of the mind's eye,' which saw colors and images dance across the stage of his consciousness.

The last sound he heard by the sense of hearing, came via Samantha's lips. "Initiating entry to target mind."

The surrounding light dimmed and darkness closed in on him. For several moments, he thought death had intervened but the darkness did not last long. A brilliant flash of intense light surged across his internal vision to explode into thousands of tiny sparks, blanking out all sensation and perception.

Then with slow escalation, the indigo hue returned, inspiring a feeling of freedom from the need for physical effort and he found himself moving along at a terrifying speed, bodiless, with a total absence of friction. The most magnificent colors flashed by as the avatar rocketed down a long tunnel into oblivion. The velocity increased until everything became a blur and then with a sudden jolt to the senses, the speed dropped to produce the sensation of floating in a void. Then a clear, velvety voice spoke.

"Hello, Professor. How are you feeling?"

Lucas's mind wouldn't compute and it took a second before he realized the computer had addressed him.

"I'm feeling fine. Thanks, Echo."

"I'm glad you're doing good. Did you enjoy the display, Professor?"

"Magnificent. This out of the body experience takes some getting used to, though."

The avatar chuckled. *"Indeed, Professor. It's a bit like being a ghost who arrives at a party with no 'body' to go with."*

The joke threw him for a brief moment, until Samantha's hand in setting up Echo's personality, clearly demonstrated itself.

"Where are we, exactly?" asked Lucas.

"We are approaching the memory banks in Gracie's cerebrum, Professor. I understand you are looking for the last memories she experienced?"

"I want to get to a place just prior to that—she read the final pages of Veronica's diary. There may be some vital clues regarding her sister's conversation with the murderer."

"I am sending out an immediate probe to locate the area, Professor. There are trillions of cells involved and we need to find the correct path."

"Thanks, Echo. I'll just sit back and see what I can see."

"I expect no more from a man who has been relegated to the quantum level, operating on half a brain, Professor."

Had the situation not been so frightening and tense Lucas would have laughed, however, he threw back his own brand of quirky humor. "You sound very much like Sam, Echo. She operates with only half a brain under normal conditions."

"Glad to see you have retained your sense of humor, Professor."

"You're welcome," answered Lucas.

The indigo hue started to change into a deep red. In theory, he understood the colors of cells would range over the visible light spectrum, dependent on the age of the memory. Red appeared to be the oldest memories and as the avatar floated by, he saw Gracie's childhood impressions.

From his perception, the 'tree' arrangement of the particular memory bank the avatar perused stretched out in front of him with branches like alcoves, extended left and right on either side. Lucas could have been in a bus traveling down a suburban street with houses, and a view of each building and yard. As had been the expectation the scenes took on holographic images of people moving in circumstances, as they had in past real life situations.

The two faces of adults loomed looking down on him and he realized it to be Gracie's view of her parents as she first saw them through her own eyes. They smiled at her, their eyes large with eyebrows raised and then laughed as she responded.

"We are years away from our intended target memories, Echo. How long will it take for the probe to establish the bank we need?"

"I'm working on it, Professor. The probe is scanning as large an area of cells as possible. As one who has never parented children, you should sit back and relax—watch how much effort goes into it."

"I really don't need to know about that side of life, thank you. It will never happen to me," said Lucas.

"You know what they say about famous last words, Professor."

"Spare me, Echo. Let's just concentrate on the work at hand."

"As you wish, O' Great One."

More memories of Gracie's childhood reeled off and the avatar picked up speed. It veered off with a sudden, violent swerve, to careen down another corridor. Lucas noticed the subtle change in the deep red hue around him. The avatar slowed, momentarily, which gave him a quick look at the scenes. A young child of about four years of age received a scolding, with the resultant tears of anguish, followed by the loving, caressing arms of her mother. All floated by his field of view and as he cast his attention to the opposite side of the avenue, the presentation of a new baby filled his vision. He knew it had to be Veronica and a sadness filled his heart.

The avatar took off at breakneck speed again and the scenes all meshed into a haze of people, actions, and circumstances.

"I believe the probe has found the relevant memories, Professor. Hold onto your hat and we'll get you there in a jiffy, via the particle express, of course." ∞∞

8

Gracie Beauchamp

The two guards seemed at ease and the man in the white coat, most likely a doctor leaned back in his chair, with eyes closed. It would appear nobody expected any trouble and the consequent need for their services relegated to a mere token of presence. Bob knew he shouldn't wait too long before he made his move. If the Internet article proved correct, there would be some sort of apparatus in the lab, which could facilitate a search of Gracie's memories.

He knew the operation would still be somewhere in its beginning stages, whatever those were. He checked his watch—only fifty minutes elapsed since he left to pick up the ordinance he required. The operating staff would have needed to set up the patient and do a certain amount of preparatory work before the experiment could begin.

Another furtive glance assured him the two guards did not take their job very seriously. One yawned cavernously while the other appeared to be reading emails, or texts, on his phone. The doctor, sitting in the chair opposite the lab entrance, looked to be asleep. Bob removed the first canister from the side pocket of his jacket and released the pin. It operated like a hand grenade and once he let go of the suppression lever, toxic gas would begin to billow out.

He hoped to catch the two guards by surprise and incapacitate them before they could react. The canister would make a noise but beyond that, the gas was colorless and they would not realize the immediate danger, until the Kolokol-1 took effect.

Bob donned a filter-mask and slipped a pair of goggles over his eyes. These would afford him a marginal protection from the gas, while he slipped passed the incapacitated guards and into the lab. He glanced around the corner once again and threw the canister into the corridor.

*

The scenes of Gracie's memories started to blur again as the avatar took off with a vengeance. Lucas felt every bit of his substance start to strip away as colors changed rapidly through the spectrum: orange, yellow, and green merged into a single mix of light-brown as the avatar streaked around corners, accelerated down corridors, and whisked through branches of memory trees, which yielded their secrets too swiftly for him to comprehend.

A slight jarring of the pictures before him brought the avatar to a sudden stop. The color changed to a light hue of violet and Lucas found himself ensconced in the midst of a scene inside a room.

A bookshelf appeared in front of him and a hand reached up to remove a book from the top shelf. Lucas read its title through the eyes of the observer, 'Culinary Principles,' who replaced it after a cursory glance. The scanning of more titles followed until, on one of the middle shelves the same hand pulled out another book, with a worn cover and opened it—

the hand, he understood, belonged to Gracie. He could see Veronica's neat handwriting through Gracie's eyes.

I met this cute guy tonight; said his name was Bob, I don't remember his last name, but we instantly clicked. He offered to see me home and I invited him to stay for a drink. We both drank a little too much—he seemed quite melancholic and talked about duty in Afghanistan. I think he is troubled by things that happened to him there....

To my surprise he started to cry and said someone was blackmailing him to be involved in a plot, to assassinate the President.... I don't think he meant to tell me because he suddenly changed his tune and told me to forget all about what he had said. But what if it's true! He left soon after that. I hope I'll see him again.

"Is what I'm reading being recorded, Echo?"

"Your every thought is being recorded, Professor."

"It only confirms what we already know, except for a few details."

"And what are these details you have so succinctly detected, o' wise and regal tutor?"

"Gracie didn't mention to Lieutenant Dunmore her friend was being blackmailed. She only said he was involved in a possible assassination attempt."

"What else did you detect, Professor?"

"He's a war veteran. This is a huge help."

"What does it mean for your case?"

"It means there are a few possibilities for motive. The vendetta against the President is not a personal issue for the killer. I suspect he will have a record which implicates him in something of importance during the war, which might be of use, to a blackmailer."

"I'm sure the FBI will be pleased to learn about these possibilities," said Echo.

"We're done here—can you move us to the memory of the attack?"

"Absolutely, my King."

Again, the avatar lurched forward and gathered speed. This time it was of short duration with a few memories of Gracie's work-life and offices, at the Political Arrow the magazine she worked for, in between. The scene before Lucas played out in a bright violet color, which indicated the memory to be very recent and one of the last she developed, before the onset of her comatose state.

A different apartment this time drew his attention to a knock on the door and Gracie moved toward it with haste. She opened the door and Lucas peered out to see a man, standing on the threshold. Before the door could be slammed shut, the figure pushed into the hallway, knocking Gracie down. Lucas experienced a sudden lurch and a view of the ceiling came into the picture.

The swift movement of the attacker did not give Lucas time to get a good look at the face. The man turned and closed the door behind him. Lucas's view of the attacker became blurred and he realized Gracie's consciousness,

because of the blow the attacker delivered to her jaw, had started to wane.

The attacker grabbed her throat and started to choke her violently and Lucas sensed the words flash across his mind: *"Where's the diary?"*

The attacker repeated it several times. For a brief moment, she looked directly into the killer's eyes and then managed to turn her head toward the desk upon which the book rested. Gracie's head lurched violently as the killer wrenched her neck in an effort to break it.

Again Lucas sensed a cracking of bones and the attacker let her go. She flopped down, out of his grasp, onto the floor and all Lucas could see from then onward was the ceiling, until it blurred and went blank.

Lucas felt as though his life had drained out of him. The face of the killer, now indelibly imprinted on his mind, continued to leer at him, despite Gracie's loss of consciousness. The violent nature of the attack left him stunned and

in a panic. It was as though the murderer had tried to kill him personally and he felt as much of a victim as Gracie Beauchamp.

He screamed at the avatar. "Get me out of here, now! I can't take this—it's too awful for words."

Darkness overcame him and after, what seemed like an eternity, Lucas heard Echo's voice coaxing him to garner his thoughts. *"Wake up, Professor. Are you okay?"*

He responded half-heartedly. "Yeah. I can hear you, Echo."

"I'm sorry, Professor. I should have warned you. It was a pretty graphic scene."

"It was more than graphic. I swear I felt the bugger's hands around my throat. I saw his despicable face." Lucas knew he had been severely rattled because he seldom, if ever, swore.

"Have you seen enough, Professor?"

"Take me back to reality, where I belong. I never want to live through something like that again."

"Aye, aye, my captain."

With a sudden show of brilliant light the surroundings suddenly disappeared and Lucas found himself surrounded by darkness. The forward motion of the avatar slowed and then stopped.

"Echo, what's happened, why aren't we moving?"

"Gracie Beauchamp's brain has suddenly stopped functioning. I think she has passed away, Professor."

*

The canister rolled down the corridor to land close to the doctor who opened his eyes and peered inquisitively at it. One of the guards jerked his head around and addressed the doctor. "Did you drop something, Doctor?"

The doctor continued staring at the canister uncomprehendingly, not sure where it came from. The canister, made of a light plastic substance made little noise in its journey, which ended three feet from his chair.

"No, it wasn't me. Damned if I know where it came from." He looked up to see if the object had fallen from the ceiling.

"What are you talking about?" asked the guard.

The doctor contemplated his answer and then went silent. His head sank to his chest and it became clear something inconsistent with the surroundings had taken place.

The guard stepped away from the door, toward the slumped man in the chair. "Are you okay, sir? Doctor?"

He smelled the gas and immediately knew they were in trouble. He shouted to the other guard. "Quick, get inside the lab."

The warning came too late. Both the men buckled over, and their weapons made a clattering noise as they fell to the floor.

Bob moved quickly. He pulled the parabellum from his pocket and jumped over the inert body of one of the guards, to reach the lab door. Wrenching it open, he stormed in with gun outstretched, to secure the target. The faces of O'Malley, Samantha and the dean, all registered shock as Bob leveled his weapon at them. He recognized O'Malley from his visit to the hospital and shouted. "If you want to live, freeze!"

O'Malley froze along with the other two. Samantha's eyes grew large as she realized their predicament. The dean stood, frozen to the spot. O'Malley considered taking his chances and drawing his weapon but he knew there would be a very slim chance of getting off a shot at their assailant. The fourth person, besides Gracie, sat immobile in a chair, hooked up to the apparatus. Bob swiveled his head slightly and saw Gracie, strapped into the gurney with the harness attached. She never stood a chance. He shot her through the head, and as he pulled the trigger, the FBI agent went for his revolver.

O'Malley had the Glock revolver halfway out of its holster under his left arm, when the attacker's second bullet tore into his shoulder and knocked him down with force. The revolver went flying and Samantha screamed. It ended seconds later as Bob made his exit, to leave the others in a state of confusion. O'Malley tried to get up but his arm hung limply and collapsed, as he tried to use it to push up off the floor. The dean didn't move. His face reflected pure horror as Samantha overcame inertia and went to O'Malley's aid.

Throughout the entire event, Lucas sat, unsighted in his chair, his left-brain consciousness trying to gather the sounds and impressions in the room. He couldn't move any part of his body and the relevant hemisphere, missing its counterpart's full participation, groped for answers.

Due to the quantum entanglement phenomenon he retained an element of lucidity on both ends but because the right brain, ensconced in the avatar focused on a new set of stimuli, the left hemisphere struggled to distinguish the noises in the room. He did not know why, but fear engulfed him and his body broke out in perspiration.

The fear became so intense, it found transmission to the avatar, and the right-brained Lucas knew something awful had happened.

∞∞

9

After the Shooting

Samantha helped a shaky O'Malley onto his feet. The dean overcame his immobilization and helped her support the agent's weight, until they managed to seat him on a spare chair against the lab wall.

"Dillon? Are you okay?" asked Samantha. Her voice trembled with emotion and tears welled up in her eyes.

"I'll live. Get my phone out of my pocket—I need to make a call."

The dean ventured to the door and looked into the corridor. The two guards, still lying on the floor, both gagged for air and rubbed their eyes, as they regained full consciousness.

"What was that?" The guard, who initially stepped over to check the canister, managed to

raise himself onto knees, which still would not support him.

"It's a type of knock-out gas," spluttered the other guard.

"Bastard caught us by surprise. I think we're fired," said the first guard.

With swollen eyes the doctor also came around and stared at the two men. "Where am I," he said.

The dean could see no sign of the assailant and stepped into the corridor.

"Did you get a look at him?"

The guard, now back on his feet, picked up his weapon and checked it. "No, sir. He wore some sort of mask, like a surgeon wears for surgery. I only caught a glimpse, before my lights went out."

O'Malley, sufficiently recovered, looked into the hallway. "I've called for backup but he'll have got clean away by now."

"And the patient?" asked the doctor, who stood on shaky legs and pushed passed O'Malley, into the lab.

"I'm afraid he got to her," said Samantha. She stood at the bedside and gazed down at Gracie with large, horror-stricken eyes. A neat hole between the patient's eyes confirmed the prognosis. "She's dead."

Then it dawned on the neuroscientist. "Oh my God. Lucas is still with the avatar. I must try to get him back."

She ran to the console where the keyboard sat and began typing in instructions with furious intensity. O'Malley came up alongside her and observed. The screen showed long horizontal lines, backed by a fuzzy static. The professor sat in the chair with harness still attached, his eyes closed and mouth open. His tongue, which lolled to one side, protruded from his mouth slightly and the pallor of his skin, appeared a whiter shade of pale.

"Where is he at the moment?" asked O'Malley.

"His right-brain consciousness is trapped as a part of the avatar and the left-hand brain is trying to work out what's happening. I'm not really sure," said Samantha.

"Can you get him back?"

"I think so, but I'm not even sure of that," Samantha answered.

*

Bob ran like the wind. He headed down the corridor to the foyer and took another hallway, which lead to the side exit. Once outside the building, he fled through the gardens using the shrubs and trees as cover until he reached the boundary wall, which separated the grounds from the street. People who started to arrive at the Institute took little notice of him as he negotiated the low wall and hurried toward the street corner. Traffic passed by, oblivious to the murderer as he crossed the road to his truck and drove away.

Later, when the police questioned Institute members about the fleeing fugitive, none could give an accurate description of the man, seen leaving the grounds early that morning. One person, however, said she saw a man step out onto the sidewalk, from the Institute grounds.

The woman, a student, said she had been busy crossing the road when he climbed over the low boundary wall opposite her. She caught a side view of the face and described the man's camouflage jacket and the blue denim jeans he wore. A forensic artist drew a composite sketch which the police distributed amongst their many on-duty officers.

Nothing about the death of Gracie Beauchamp was mentioned in the news. Members of the Institute saw an ambulance leave the grounds but only guessed as to its real purpose.

Twenty minutes later, Bob dumped the old truck in a deserted area and called for a taxi to take him home. With his mission successfully accomplished, he called the local police to report the truck stolen and then relaxed on the back verandah of the apartment with a cup of coffee. The adrenaline still coursed through his system to bring a tremble to the hand which held the coffee mug. Half an hour later, he glanced at his watch and decided to get ready for the afternoon's detail.

*

Samantha sat at the console and continued to key in instructions, while O'Malley met with the paramedics in the corridor. They examined his arm and after determining the bullet had exited with minor damage to tissue, they bandaged him up and supplied a sling. Lucas still sat without any movement, his face a deathly white and mouth still half open. The FBI special agent returned to the lab and came to stand behind Samantha. "Any luck, Sam?"

For once she didn't have a snarky remark. "Nothing so far—judging by the entry point of the murderer's bullet, its passage would have narrowly missed the cerebrum area. I'm hoping there has been no physical disruption to the avatar in order for it to have a chance of negotiating a safe passage toward the exit point."

"What would be happening inside Gracie's brain?" asked O'Malley.

"Without her brain functioning there would be no electrical stimulation for the cells to work, no propagation of messages through the dendrites and across the synaptic gaps. The only hope lies in the inner layer of the cytoskeletal structure, a substance we call tubulin, which has quantum properties, to assist the probes sent out by Echo."

O'Malley scratched his temple. "When will we know the avatar has returned?"

"When Lucas opens his eyes," she said.

The dean arrived after a short visit to the reception and consultation with his secretary. "Are we making any progress?" he asked.

O'Malley answered. "Sam's doing her best to get the professor back to us. In the meantime, we need to secure the area—no one is allowed in here until all this has been sorted out."

"I've already anticipated that requirement, Special Agent. The area is off limits to everyone and we have cordoned off the corridor on both sides. Your two guards will enforce it."

Don Hadley, the FBI Assistant Director, arrived and O'Malley excused himself. "Keep me updated, Sam."

She gave him a glance but didn't answer.

Hadley walked over to the gurney and looked down at Gracie. "I think we might be in deep shit over this," he said.

O'Malley raised his eyebrows. "The two guards were caught completely by surprise. No one expected any trouble."

"I guess the killer must have been watching our movements all the time, Dillon. I won't say anything to the director until we know more about the situation."

O'Malley explained the professor's precarious position.

"Oh, for God's sake, this is getting worse. You had better hope he makes it."

O'Malley flared up. "It's not my head on the chopping block, Don. You and the judge made the decision to force the institute to comply."

"Take it easy. We're only trying to do our jobs, here. The judge won't be happy when he hears we allowed Gracie to be murdered, but ultimately he takes responsibility."

O'Malley's demeanor cooled but he still felt upset by the assistant director's earlier remark. "I just need a rest," he said.

"How's your arm?"

"I'll live," said O'Malley.

"Let me know what transpires."

O'Malley nodded and the boss left.

Samantha turned her head. "I think I might be getting a response from the avatar."

The agent moved quickly to her side. He leaned in toward her, their eyes focused on the screen and a delicate perfume wafted up to greet his olfactory senses. The skin on her neck, white and delicate, posed a stark contrast to the deep pink dye of her hair and he felt irresistibly drawn to her. Even the six metal rings, which pierced her earlobe, provided a measure of unsophisticated embellishment to the otherwise groovy appearance.

"What's happening, Sam?"

She pointed to a spot on the screen. "Do you see this thin, red line here? This is an electrical impulse, seeking a route through the configuration of cells via the inner walls of the skeletal conduit. All this, over here, represents the cerebrum tissue and the probe is emanating from this area." She pointed to another spot on the screen.

"If you say so. It's just neuro-speak to me at this point. Is the avatar moving?"

"Very slowly. It appears the probes are trying to find the exit point."

"Can you speak to Echo?" asked O'Malley.

"I am trying to establish contact but there's a lack of continuity for signal propagation."

*

All Lucas saw dark silhouettes all around him. Although his focus remained glued to the immediate surroundings, the cold eyes of the killer still haunted him and he could almost feel the hands around his throat. Everything became reduced to fine details and the consequences of Gracie's sudden passing would not create a synergy with these refinements.

He understood this aspect of his thoughts. The right brain reduced everything to detail and he could not, for the life of him, contemplate the greater aspect of his dilemma. He knew, deep within—somewhere—there had to be a ramification to the end of all brain function, but it became obscured by the right hemisphere's point of view.

"Where are we, Echo?"

"*We are entrenched inside a cytoskeletal sheath and moving very slowly, Professor.*"

"Are we still in the memory bank?"

"*We are, Professor. I am sending out as many probes as possible, but the sheath tubulin is causing too great a proliferation of the signals and confusing the transmissions.*"

"Surely some of the cell bodies would still be lingering, even after death?"

"*I agree, Professor, but to find one that still maintains a measure of activity will be difficult and it may not lie along the exit route.*"

"I remember clinical studies on brain activity, after immediate death, revealing continuity for several minutes. This was reported in many case studies. There has to be cells and axons working for this to be a reality."

"You are correct, Professor. This is precisely what we are looking for. I'm sure we'll find something, but there is little time left."

"Probe for a high amount of DMT. This also proved to be the case at the moment of death."

"Dimethyltryptamine is being detected as we speak, Professor. I'm hoping it will be sufficient to help us discover a sheath, which contains a still-active soma."

Lucas realized there wasn't much more to be done. He needed to let the avatar get on with things. They would know soon enough.

An eternity passed before Echo's next response. *"We have an active soma with a linking axon, Professor."*

The avatar lurched sideways into a new corridor and began to pick up a small measure of speed. A dim, violet luminescence glowed on the surroundings and Lucas could make out impressions of swirling nebulous clouds, which became darker as the avatar progressed.

"What are these nebula-like formations, Echo?"

"*I believe they are impressions of great pain. Emotional turmoil, mixed with physical pain.*"

"Could this be the pain attached to the mind's final realization that life is slipping away?"

"*It is possible, my king.*"

Lucas fell silent in the contemplation of what he saw and an emotion slid across the landscape of his awareness. It felt like a mixture of pity and guilt surrounded by a sea of sadness.

The avatar lurched again. "What's happening, Echo?"

"*We have found a stronger cell body and this one's leading us in the right direction.*"

Lucas continued his vigil. The avatar moved much quicker and the illumination increased as they raced along the axon, but seconds later, it bucked like a bronco and jerked violently to the left. Forward momentum slowed to a crawl and indescribable fear welled up within him as darkness fell with sudden bellicosity.

Echo's voice filtered through to his awareness. *"Stay calm, Professor—we have exited the axon, which appears to be severed, for reasons unknown."*

This puzzled Lucas. "The axon has been severed? Through what medium is the avatar making its way?"

"I don't know the reason, Professor, but a large gap has appeared in Gracie's brain. It's as though a foreign object has plowed through the cortex and made a large aperture."

"This is highly unusual," said Lucas.

"Fortunately, the aperture is acting as a frictionless conduit, making it possible to continue a forward motion."

In the semi-darkness, Lucas could see more nebulous clouds form around the avatar as it started to move again. Then with an awful, gut-wrenching jar, everything came to a sudden standstill. Familiar sounds, which included the smell of a clinical process, filtered through to his senses, and Lucas's eyes flew open to see a smiling face—Samantha.

∞∞

10

Back to the First lady

The first lady's speech at the school went off without a hitch. As usual, the security assigned to such functions included four secret service agents who performed a meticulous threat assessment on the detail. The presidential couple's youngest child, one of the school's attendees, proudly performed the task of co-host with the school principal. After the talk at the school, the agents whisked Sheila Lewis back to the White House where she would rest up for the afternoon, before attending an evening function with her husband.

Agent Coulson saw her to the door of the presidential suite. "Is there anything I can get for you, ma'am?" he asked.

"No, thank you, Agent Coulson, but there is something I would like you to do for me."

"Just name it, ma'am."

"I want you to check in the security detail log where the presidential SUV stopped yesterday in lower Manhattan. It will be an apartment complex. I also want you to find out who lives there."

"I'm not supposed to divulge such information without the consent of the chief of staff, ma'am."

"I know the rules, Agent. But this is very important to me and I am calling in a favor here. I have given you glowing conduct reports since your admission to this detail. It's these reports that will lead to an eventual promotion for you. No one will know you gave me the information and it's really a small thing I'm asking."

Coulson considered the situation for a moment. He understood why the first lady required the information and knew it could lead to a possible breach of protocol on his behalf. He didn't like the president and considered it fortunate he had not been deployed on the man's security detail, but to pass on the information could lead to trouble for all the president's personal security guards. It would be unlikely, however, for the deed to be traced back to him personally.

"Yes, ma'am. Give me a few minutes. and I'll be back."

Coulson walked along the hallway to the empty duty office and sat at the duty officer's desk. The president's travel log could be accessed through the local intranet with the same code each agent used for viewing the upcoming details of security appointments. He found the relevant information without any difficulty, made a note of the address and picked up the phone to dial a number in the New York City utility department. After a few minutes he hung up and returned to the presidential suite.

Sheila Lewis opened the door and smiled. "That was quick. What do you have?"

"Her name is Rosemary Banks. She's a stripper at a nightclub in Queens. Age twenty-eight years."

"Thank you, Agent Coulson. You've been most helpful. That'll be all."

"Happy to be of help, ma'am."

Sheila closed the door and walked to the sitting room to pour a martini. In her mind there could be no mistake, regarding her husband's infidelity. Highly agitated, she mumbled aloud. "So, Martin. I'm not good enough for you. You need some young floozy to make you feel good."

The tears started to stream down her face. "Oh God, what am I going to do? I feel so trapped."

The martini helped to calm her and after two more, she walked unsteadily to her bedroom, lay down on the bed and fell into a fitful sleep.

*

"Wake up, sleepyhead. Welcome to the real world."

Lucas stared with glassy eyes at Samantha's face. It took a few moments for him to regain all his senses and remember where he was.

"Your eye-makeup's smudged," he said.

"Connect with the other half of your brain, sweet-pea. You're still seeing only details."

Her smile disappeared, to be replaced with a concerned look. "You nearly didn't make it back, Luke. I thought for a moment my life would be spent working with a half-brained professor."

Another face peered at him as Samantha removed the harness from his head. "Welcome, weary traveler. How are feeling?" asked the dean.

"With my hands, as usual," he answered.

"I see you've not lost your humor, Lucas," said the dean. "We thought you were a gonner."

"Thanks to Sam's brain child, Echo, we managed quite well. I have things to tell you," returned Lucas.

O'Malley entered the lab and saw the three scientists talking. "I see you made it back to home base, Professor."

Lucas turned his head and eyed O'Malley. "I'm glad to report the mission to be a success, Dillon. We need to talk, but first I want to know what happened to Gracie."

Samantha teared up as O'Malley answered. "Gracie was shot."

Lucas closed his eyes. "I knew something terrible had happened."

He went on to explain the sudden change in the avatar's forward flight and the aperture which opened up, to provide the final push for the exit point.

"I couldn't figure it out at the time but it's clear now," he said.

O'Malley shared the news of the attack by the killer. "Unfortunately, our two guys at the door were caught napping and the killer surprised us. I caught a bullet for trying to pull out my revolver when he shot Gracie. He got clean away and a manhunt has, so far, found nothing."

"Let's talk about what you saw, or do you need rest. Are you up to it?"

"I'm certainly knackered but now that I can think with a whole brain again, I feel invigorated. It will be a little while before the program is able to decode the holographic record of my thoughts and I feel there is something the FBI can follow up on in the meantime."

"There's coffee in the pot if you're thirsty, O' great one," said Samantha.

"You and Echo sound like identical twins," said Lucas.

She poured the coffee and placed the mug in his hands. He took a sip and made a face. "One of your typical lab concoctions, no doubt."

O'Malley and the dean looked at each other and shook their heads.

Lucas steeled himself to begin. "The journey was everything we thought it might be, and more, but I'll get to the point. Veronica's diary proved useful. Some things she mentioned should help us track down the killer." He paused.

O'Malley, Samantha, and the dean leaned closer, eager to hear what he had to say.

"The killer did time in Afghanistan, on active duty, and could be suffering from PTSD. Veronica mentioned he spoke of things that worried him. A second fact of importance is the killer is being blackmailed to be involved in the assassination of the president."

O'Malley digested the information and looked thoughtfully at Lucas. "We know the man's name is Bob—short for Robert. He must have been involved in some sort of important action which brought on the PTSD symptoms. We will need to check out all veterans with the first name of Robert, who have recently returned from deployment and who might have known symptoms of the disorder."

"I asked Echo to probe the scene of Gracie's attack in the hope of seeing the killer's face. This was the most frightening and heart-wrenching experience of the entire trip."

"Well, don't keep us in suspense, my king," said Samantha.

Lucas lowered his chin and looked at the floor. "I won't forget the eyes. The irises were a frightening, darkish, almost black, color. I swear, if I ever have to look into those eyes again, I will kill the bastard."

"Shit, sweetie. That's hard-talk for you," said Samantha.

The dean raised his eyebrows and O'Malley narrowed his eyelids.

"So you got a look at the killer's face? I will need to have a forensic artist sit with you and make a portrait. How long before the program can convert the holo-files?" O'Malley asked.

Samantha batted her eyelids at him. "About twenty-four hours, ducky."

"I'm going to talk to the military. We need to follow up on the clues as quickly as possible. I'll be back when the files are available—I'd love to see what the inside of a brain looks like," said O'Malley.

"Only if I can hold your hand. You might crap your pants, Mister FBI man."

O'Malley shook his head in exasperation. "I've called for the coroner to send a vehicle for Gracie. We've discovered she and Veronica were both from a foster home and have no contact with the people who looked after them. The office is still trying to track down any surviving relatives from the original family. They appear to have had a brother, who also went through the foster care system but no one knows where he lives, or if he is even still alive."

The mention of Gracie toned down Samantha's quirky humor and they gazed at the gurney. "You need to remove the harness," said Lucas.

She stepped to the gurney and looked down at the dead girl's face. "She looks so peaceful now."

After a few moments, she pulled the harness off and moved the equipment out of the way before pulling the sheet over Gracie's head.

The dean held out his hand to Lucas. "You should get onto your feet. The next few hours will be a test for you as the brain refocuses and creates a synergy once again. I think Samantha should stay with you for a while."

Lucas frowned. "I'm sure I'll be okay."

"Aunty Sam's coming to your place and spending the night—on the sofa, of course, and I won't take no for an answer."

Lucas grumbled under his breath and took the dean's hand. Back on his feet, the room began to swirl with a sudden vengeance and he sagged onto the chair.

"Don't say we didn't warn you, tiger," said Samantha.

Lucas shut his eyes for a few moments to stop the room from turning. O'Malley shook his head. "I'll leave you to it, then. The coroner should be here in a few minutes. He won't ask any questions. Just allow him in for a brief examination and he will remove the body."

Tears welled up in Samantha's eyes, again. The dean pulled out a handkerchief and handed it to her and gestured toward Lucas. "Don't worry, my dear. It's been a rough day. Take technical Tom home and give him a hot toddy."

She dabbed at her eyes and gave a half giggle. "I'll do exactly that."

O'Malley moved to the door. "I'm going to say goodbye. I'll send the forensic artist around to Lucas's home, first thing tomorrow morning."

Lucas acknowledged the agent's statement and stood unsteadily to his feet with Samantha's help. "I'll be okay in a few minutes—there's no need to fuss, Sam," he said.

"That's what you say, Don Quixote. Let's go bash up another windmill."

The two limped out of the lab and down the corridor toward the side entrance to the carpark. Samantha opened the side door of Lucas's old 1939 Bentley and sat him in the front passenger seat. After securing the seatbelt, she demanded, "Keys."

Lucas reluctantly groped in his pants pocket and pulled out a set of keys. She skipped around to the driver's side and hopped in. "Yippee, at last, I get to drive Waltzing Matilda."

Lucas offered mild resistance. "Really, Sam, you should have just let me sit for another ten minutes and I would be fine."

"Fiddlesticks, Professor. Your two brains are not in synergy, yet, and won't be for several more hours. You have been through a very traumatic experience. It's time for Aunty Sam to take care of you."

The Mark Five, Bentley coupe, roared to life as Samantha turned the key in the ignition and gingerly coaxed the old gear box into reverse. The car lurched backward as she let out the clutch. "Oops. I'm not used to manual gearboxes anymore."

Lucas closed his eyes. "Take it easy on the old girl, Sam."

She rammed the box into first gear and shot off, out of the carpark. Two cars, approaching from opposite directions slammed on their brakes as the Bentley bounced heavily on its ancient suspension in negotiation of the driveway's transition and onto the road. Samantha slammed her foot on the gas and the four-and-a-quarter liter motor bellowed in response. Lucas buried his head in his hands and groaned.

"Oh, don't be such a ninny, Lucas. You treat this thing with kid's gloves, but she needs a good clearing of the exhausts and cylinders."

Lucas raised his head and glanced out of the window. "Oh, my God. I've just escaped death in someone else's brain and now I'm going to die on the road."

Samantha laughed in maniacal fashion.

∞∞

11

Blackmail letter

Bob returned from his work detail and flopped down on the sofa. With eyes closed, his mind returned to the nightmare of Afghanistan, as it always did when he tried to relax. The scene started with him giving the order to fire on the enemy, followed by the constant rattle of gunfire in his ears. It ended with the death of twenty three allied, Canadian soldiers. Bob, when later perusing the files of the dead combatants, remembered every face. Twenty three letters had gone out to the families of the victims, a miserable token of condolence, which each family received from the US War department. He amplified his own guilt a hundred fold in his mind.

On the table lay the unopened mail from the previous day which caught his attention. The end of the month loomed and bills needed to be paid but he felt unmotivated to rise off the couch and open letters. One cream-colored envelope caught his eye, however, and he decided to give it a closer inspection. The last instruction received from the blackmailer came in such an envelope. Bob's heart gave a lurch as he lifted the envelope and scrutinized it. The same untraceable print, cut-outs from a magazine or newspaper, characterized the address. With tentative fingers he opened the envelope and removed the letter from inside.

The time has come for you to be on your best behaviour and do your duty. Your next work detail will be to accompany the President and First Lady to the G7 convention on climate change, in St Louis. You will make your way to the shower room on the top floor, overlooking the main hall. In the shower room you will find and unused 180mm pipe, sticking out of the wall. It extends from the old decommissioned boiler room, next door to the showers. The pipe has a blind flange closing it off. Inside the third locker you will find an adjustable spanner on the top shelve. Undo the bolts of the blind and remove it. Inside the pipe you will find the weapon, wrapped in plastic. At exactly 11:30 pm the President of the United States will take the podium. After performing your duty there is a scaffold, erected by a window-cleaning company, via which you will make your escape from an adjacent window. You will be able to enter the building again, on the ground floor through a side door, which will be left unlocked. You must not fail, for you know what is at stake if you do. Memorize the outlay and destroy this communication.

Bob broke out in a sweat. The letter fell from his hands as he closed his eyes and contemplated what lay ahead. He didn't give a rat's ass about the President; no one did, but an assassination would lead to an intensive manhunt. The blackmailer's plans could so easily go wrong. The letter included a rough drawing of the building's outlay, with its four floors. He understood the plan—it was not complicated. The side door through which he would reenter the building led straight into the main hall and he would have to get there as quickly as possible, in order to alleviate any suspicion. There would, however, be enough turmoil which he could use to make for the stairs, in a feigned attempt to apprehend the assassin.

He moved to the fridge, took out a beer, walked onto the back verandah and sagged into a deck chair.

*

O'Malley looked out the window of his fourth floor office on Pennsylvania Avenue. From his vantage point in the J. Edgar Hoover Building, he could see the White House with its famous neoclassical styled portico. He loved the history of the area with its strong political fragrance and would not want to live anywhere else. Honored to be a part of the security watch for the country, O'Malley believed this to be his life's purpose and every time he looked out the window, it reminded him of his vow to honor and protect.

His arm ached a little whenever he bumped or moved it but the healing process appeared to be well underway. Don Hadley, the assistant

director sat opposite the desk, busy on his cell phone. The call, to the chairman of the

Joint Chiefs, promised to raise a little bit of a furor for them, but needless to say, the FBI required the military's cooperation. Very few people were read into the possible assassination plot but the Chairman had been one of them. Hadley closed his eyes and listened to the chairman's response to his request.

With a role of the eyes for O'Malley's benefit, Hadley grabbed a millisecond lull in the chairman's tirade to launch into an explanation. "Listen to me, Peter, I know there are protocols and rules regarding the release of military records but for Christ's sake, this is a possible assassination attempt we're looking at —you know that."

The chairman's rant started up again. Hadley pulled the phone away from his ear and gave it a long stare. O'Malley smiled to himself. The records the FBI needed were not classified documents. The real problem lay in the competition between the top brass of the four main departments. It appeared they clashed over information sharing. The CIA and NSA had the same problem with the Military. It made him sick to the stomach.

Hadley, with a final attempt at persuading the Chairman, threatened to get the President to intervene. This appeared to be a reasonable weapon because the chairman started to back pedal with excuses and then, with a final salvo of expletives, acquiesced. The assistant director returned his phone to its pocket and gazed at O'Malley. "We'll have the records of every soldier, with the first name of Robert, who has been involved in action and suffered symptoms of PTSD, within three hours."

"Good. I can never understand these military types. You would think we were asking them to give us their personal banking details."

Hadley stood and stretched. "The two guys who messed up at the lab—have you dealt with the matter?"

O'Malley looked at his hands. "Yeah—I take some of the blame myself. I should have expected trouble. It's a tragedy when you think about it. Two lovely young girls, cut down so early in their careers. I hope we catch this bastard."

Hadley looked thoughtful. "I can't but help think this goes a lot deeper than one or two people. If we can catch this guy it would be great to employ the same method and find out who he's involved with, a lot of bad stuff could be cleaned out of the way."

O'Malley agreed. "I'm not sure if the Professor will be that keen to do it again. We're okay as long as the press is not brought into it. What did the judge say?"

"There will be an enquiry into Gracie's actual cause of death but for the time being we're safe with regard to the memory intrusion. The Hospital signed over responsibility to the FBI and will not see the body again. The State Coroner has agreed to leave the cause of death as murder, stemming from the original assault."

"I guess a lot will depend on how efficient the Memory Sweeper is. I believe it's a brilliant

breakthrough and I can't see any problem with its use in crime detection," said O'Malley.

Hadley snorted. "Until the liberal mindset is applied to it and we're threatened with law suits involving invasion of privacy."

He moved to the door. "Let me know what you find regarding the Military records."

O'Malley looked out the window again. "It may take a little time but I'll put two of my brightest agents on it."

Hadley walked off along the corridor and left O'Malley to think. He picked up his phone and dialed home.

"I'll be home in half an hour, honey. Is there anything you need?"

Janet responded with a request for a pint of milk and O'Malley closed the office door to head off to the parking garage. A half-hour later he arrived home with milk in hand. When Janet saw his one arm in a sling, she froze.

"What on earth happened to you?"

O'Malley gingerly removed his jacket and hung it on the coat hook at the door.

"I took stray bullet in the course of duty this morning—it passed clean through with little tissue damage—nothing to worry about."

"I know I shouldn't even ask how it happened but you could have been killed," she said.

"Let's not talk about it, Jan. These things happen."

She glared at him. "You mean, we must sweep it under the rug and forget it ever happened—like everything else in our lives?"

"You know I don't mean that, love. It's just I don't want to talk about it right now. I need a drink."

She moved to the liquor cabinet and poured him a whisky as he sat on the settee. "You never talk about anything anymore," she said.

"I'm sorry, sweetheart but now's not the right time for us to resurrect this argument."

"There never seems to be a right time, Dillon. When are you going to realize our marriage is in trouble because you can't stop blaming yourself for Fallon's death?"

*

Sheila Lewis sat in the armchair and waited for her husband to come in from the Oval Office. His usual time of appearance ranged between 6:30 and 8:00 p.m. A lot depended on what crisis the country, or one of its allies, faced and she became used to times of not seeing him for the entire night. It came with the job and at least she knew he would be in his office. It's when he took his little jaunts away from the White House that she worried about his infidelity. She knew what should be said but wasn't sure if she could do it without creating a scene. Martin Lewis was a complicated man—brilliant but unpredictable.

At times she thought she might let it go but to do so would be, in the long run, to her detriment. Sheila doubted she still loved him. A long history of control and subtle abuse followed from their early marriage years to the present day. The prestige and access to the finer things in life tempered her occasional desire to ask for a divorce and now that Martin was the most powerful man in the free-world, to complicate his life with such proceedings, would be almost impossible. At times he could be quite congenial and even tender but it never lasted. Martin had developed the reputation of being the most unpopular president of the modern era but despite this image he managed the world stage with effectiveness. Even his most ardent critics would have to agree. The respect America now received from its adversaries, rivaled the sentiment at the end of World War Two.

The door opened and the President marched in after shouting a goodbye to his Chief of Staff. Sheila steeled herself to confront him, as she stood to peck his cheek.

"Hey, honey—have a good day?" he asked.

She smiled wanly and allowed him to pass on his way to the liquor cabinet.

"I guess it was okay, Martin. I have a question I want to ask you."

He ignored her statement. "Are you packed for St Louis, Tomorrow?" he asked.

She nodded and waited for him to pour a drink. "Am I drinking alone?" he ventured.

"Martin—who is Rosemary Banks?"

∞∞

12

Samantha, the Nurse

With the Bentley parked in the garage downstairs Samantha busied herself in getting Lucas settled for the night. Ignoring his objections she filled the bath with hot water and proceeded to strip off his clothes. On wobbly legs he stood before her, conscious of his nakedness. Lucas, with his brain not yet firing on all cylinders, felt no real compulsion to stop her but did manage to compute an acute awareness of his vulnerable position. Who knew what would happen if their hormones took over.

She helped him step over the rim of the bath and he sank down into the warm, soapy water

with gratitude, more to hide his private parts from her steady gaze. They had never ventured this far in their tenuous relationship, but some close encounters, where lips poised to kiss or hands positioned to explore, became derailed due to factors beyond their under-standing. Either Lucas remembered some lost thought regarding an experiment or, as in one circumstance at Samantha's apartment one of her many cats strayed across the boundary of their adventurousness, to disrupt the action.

Lucas could not quite put everything to-gether and appeared to be floating on a cloud of confusion. At times, complete lucidity capti-vated his thinking but the moment lasted for only a few seconds, before the details of the killer's eyes would be right in his face, again. At times he experienced the motion of the avatar, in a headlong rush toward the memory banks and then the sudden jerk, followed by a lurch as it rounded obstacles and changed di-rection, into new corridors. A queasiness, from motion sickness, niggled at the bottom of his gut.

"Come, sweetie. It's time to get out of the bath and get you into bed," said Samantha.

"Have you washed every part of me?"

"Every contour of your magnificent frame, honey."

She helped him out of the bath and began to dry him off with a towel. "I like that," he said.

He sat on the edge of the bath while she toweled his back and reveled in the rub and massage of his muscles. When Samantha perceived his body to be sufficiently dried she assisted him into the bedroom, where he sat on the bed.

"Let's get your pajamas on," she said.

"Perhaps it's better if I left them off." He caught hold of her wrist as she reached for his sleepwear on a nearby shelf. For a moment their eyes met and he drew her close to him. She took his face in her hands and moved into position for the intended kiss to follow but it was not to be. With a sudden blaring of sound, the phone beside the bed, jangled out Cannon in D and they both withdrew in surprise. With the moment spoiled Samantha gave a deep sigh and picked it up. "Hello?"

At the other end the dean's voice tickled her ear. "Sam. I just wanted to make sure you and Lucas got home safely."

"Everything's fine. Don Quixote is just getting ready for bed. I'm taking good care of him."

They spoke for a few minutes and she hung up. A quick glance at the Professor confirmed him to have fallen asleep during the short duration of the conversation and she drew the blanket over him.

"Sleep well, my pet—perhaps another time." She turned off the light and stalked off to the bathroom.

*

In the morning Lucas felt right as reign. The night's sleep allowed all the symptoms of his epic journey to resolve and he awoke to the smell of bacon and eggs.

"Coffee?" Samantha looked into the bedroom and smiled.

"Oh yeah—smells good."

"Better get dressed. The forensic artist will be here soon," she said.

He gave her a guilty look. "Did we—? Last night?"

"Don't worry about your virginity, Professor—nothing happened. Do you think I would take advantage of you in a weakened and vulnerable state?"

"Of course you would," he joked.

She stuck her tongue out at him and pulled a face. "I am particular about whom I jump into the sack with."

"You mean I have to be human?"

"Which you're not," she quipped.

He laughed. "I see the traumatic experience of yesterday didn't dampen your ardor any."

"Come and get some bacon and eggs."

"I'll get dressed," he said.

Fifteen minutes later the Forensic artist arrived. He looked around the interior of the warehouse apartment and expressed delight at what he saw. "I have wanted to do something like this for ages—going through a nasty divorce, though."

"Sorry to hear that," said Lucas.

"Can we get on with our business. I want to get on home and then drop in at the Institute," groused Samantha.

"You can go, Sam—take the scooter. I don't need any help explaining what I saw," said Lucas.

She gave him a 'you just hurt my feelings', look.

"Sorry, Sam—I wasn't being thoughtless. I'm grateful you were able to stay here last night. I don't want to inconvenience you any further."

"It's not an inconvenience for me—I want to see what this murderer looks like."

The forensic artist coughed to indicate he was ready to sit down and start work.

"Let's sit at the table," said Lucas. They each took a seat and the artist asked several questions to which Lucas gave answers. He made a sketch on a pad and after each question he would listen to the answer and then draw the impression Lucas gave. After twenty minutes he laid the pad on the table and pushed it forward for them to see.

The Professor gasped. "That's him—great job."

Samantha picked up the pad and stared at the drawing. "You're good at this, aren't you?"

It's what they pay me to do, Ma'am."

Can I make a copy of this?" asked Lucas.

"Suit yourself. What will you do with the copies?" asked the artist.

"I have some friends who are well connected with the city. I know we'll most likely be able to quickly produce a name and address for the

killer but he might be hard to find once he knows we're after him."

Samantha stood to pick up her purse, a leather studded bag with a long strap that looked more like a pouch in which an ancient apothecary carried potent drugs. She came round the table and pecked Lucas on the cheek. "See you later, o' great one."

"Bye, Sam. The scooter's keys are in the usual place."

The artist turned to Lucas after Samantha left. "Girlfriend?"

"No—assistant," said the Professor.

The artist's cellphone rang and he pulled it from his side pocket. "Dave here?"

*

Later, Lucas parked the Bentley in downtown Manhattan and walked to Columbus Circle. He knew where to find the person whose help he needed. A group of homeless men and women stood around a small gas heater in an attempt

to stay warm in the cool November afternoon. They looked up as Lucas, dressed in jeans and a fur-lined jacket, approached. Recognition by the group came with spontaneous and loud greetings, an indication to any outsider, that they knew the professor well.

A shabby man in his early forties clapped Lucas on the back. "Greetings Professor—it's good to see you again."

A young woman in tights and a dirty sweater with holes in it sidled up and gave him a hug. "What brings you to our domain, Prof?"

Three others gathered around to welcome him into their circle around the gas heater and he stuck out his hands to the tiny flames, for warmth. "I need to talk to Shanks," he said.

They looked around at each other and the lanky man grinned. "Got some trouble, Professor?"

Lucas smiled. "Not really, but I need to find someone."

"Lost that sexy assistant of yours, Prof?" the young woman asked.

"No, Daisy—this is unfortunately serious business," said Lucas.

A voice behind them said, "Well, if it isn't my old drinking buddy."

They turned to see another homeless man, wearing an old tattered army coat and a Stoker's hat. His silver-gray hair stuck out the bottom of the hat and splayed out over a grimy, old, white shirt's collar. A grizzly growth covered the man's chin and the pupils of his red-ringed eyes, glistened as blue as a June sky.

"Hello, Shanks," said Lucas.

"To what do we owe a visit from Manhattan's greatest mind?"

Lucas laughed. "You wouldn't have said that yesterday, Shanks—but that's another story. I need your help."

"What can I, and the Panhandle Society do for you, Lucas?"

Shanks and Lucas went back a long way. The professor first discovered the homeless man twelve years prior, at death's door lying on a bench in Central Park, late one afternoon. Shanks barley survived a beating from an overzealous cop who thought he dealt in drugs. Lucas revived the homeless man who would have certainly died from his injuries, had he been left out in the elements. He helped

Shanks to the general hospital. The young medical student, in his early twenties, paid the single night's stay out of his own pocket and then took Shanks to his small apartment in Brooklyn, where the homeless man recovered fully from his injuries. From that day forward the two forged a friendship which endeared Lucas to the homeless community, all of whom soon came to know of the deed. Shanks rose amongst his peers as a man who could organize the panhandling scene at the street level and help other homeless people to survive the hardships of their lifestyle. No one knew how old he was—in his seventies, perhaps. He claimed to have fought in the Vietnam war.

"I have a sketch of a man whom I would like the folk to keep an eye out for. He is dangerous and should not be approached. The Feds and local enforcement will be looking for him too, but he might prove hard to find."

Shanks took the sketch from Lucas and scrutinized it. "Can't miss those eyes."

"He has dark hair, looks to be about thirty-five years old and has seen service in Afghanistan or Iraq."

"Got any more copies?" asked Shanks.

Lucas handed over six copies, which Shanks distributed to the others. "Let's be aware, folks. Use your contacts."

"If you find out anything call me from a booth—you have my cell number," said Lucas.

"Got any incentive for the people?" asked Shanks.

"I'll provide a bonus for the person who makes a positive identification and gets the word back to me before the police catch the guy."

After some further banter and chatter with his homeless friends Lucas left Columbus Circle and walked back to the Bentley, satisfied that the measures now in motion, would serve to make a quick apprehension of the murderer. He glanced at the time and decided to return home. Samantha would be busy with the holo-files of the memory sweep and he saw no reason to return to the Institute. The present time would be better spent setting up his notes, as regular classes were set to start on the following day. The Dean's gracious allocation of time to the development of the Sweeper assured lectures gave way for a good measure of research, for at least ten days every month.

Back at home Lucas settled down in his study with the laptop. He pulled up the lecture schedule and got to work. He knew it would not be long before the murderer slipped up. He did not realize how soon this would materialize, to send his life into overdrive.

∞∞

13

The St. Louis Detail

Agent Coulson and his colleague enjoyed the regular assignment to the First Lady's security detail. With Coulson as the lead agent they worked well as a team. Six more agents, assigned to the protection of the President, arrived in the duty room, for inclusion on the Latest St. Louis detail list. Coulson looked at the time—6:30 a.m. All of them felt the pressure, brought on by the latest intelligence report, of a potential assassination attempt. Additional agents would be joining their small force on arrival at the conference center. Air Force One waited at JFK for its most important patrons and the plan for the route would only be known, once they left the White House. The journey to St. Louis would take an hour and fifteen minutes. A special armor-plated limo would take the Presidential couple from Lambert-St. Louis Airport to the conference center in the City, the route heavily reconnoitered for any available areas, which might lend themselves to a shooter. Every precaution possible had been taken to protect the President.

The six secret service agents arrived in the duty room at 6:35 a.m. and they left in the Presidential convoy for the airport, with an entourage of security vehicles, all driving at high speed and in close formation. When Air Force One took off at 7:05 a.m., everyone breathed a sigh of relief. The real tests, however, still lay ahead.

The drive from the Lambert-St. Louis Airport to the Chesterton Complex Conference Center went off without a hitch and the agents started to relax—the time; 8:20 a.m.. The conference, scheduled for 11:30 bristled with security and Agent Coulson believed no one would be able to get into the Center with a weapon. Security had never been so well orchestrated or strictly controlled and he sat back with the others, to wait. He engaged his colleague in small-talk while dignitaries arrived to take their seats. At 11:20 a.m. Coulson's colleague stood and said, "I just need to take a quick pee, Bob—five minutes?"

Agent Coulson nodded and leaned back in his seat. "We still have ten minutes before the President's speech. All the corridors and rooms on the four floors have been checked—there's no danger we know of."

The agent walked off to the bathrooms at the back of the auditorium. The voice of the chief supervisor on the security detail spoke through the earpiece. "Everything okay where you are, Bob?"

"All's well, Chief. Dennis has just left for a quick pee. He'll be back in five."

"Very well—keep a sharp eye."

His colleague returned and sat beside him as the chairman of the National Climate Control committee, walked to the podium, to make an introduction for the President.

At 8:28 a.m., Agent Coulson leaned over to his colleague. "Keep an eye—I think I saw someone come in at the West side exit—I'm going to check it out. I'll let the chief know."

He spoke briefly into his wrist-mic and arose from his seat at the West side-door entrance to the auditorium.

*

Dillon O'Malley looked at his watch and yawned—time for another cup of coffee. The forensic artist assigned to sketch the image of the killer's face, had still not arrived despite the urgency of the threat against the President. If the Professor's condition and lucidity, on the previous evening were better, the artist could have done the sketch the previous night and they would have had the result within minutes of submitting it to the data bases. Two of O'-Malley's agents had started to work on the military records after their arrival, via the secure intranet system, which linked the most important government departments. The chairman of the Joint Chiefs promise to provide the military records requested by Hadley, came to fruition but it took a lot longer than anticipated. The number of vets, who carried the first name of Robert, and who returned home after deployment within the past months, exceeded the expected number. It would appear that at one point in time, 'Robert' had become extremely popular as a first name.

Assistant Director Hadley mentioned that the President's schedule would take him and the first Lady to St. Louis for a Climate Control conference that day. The security arrangement rated at its highest priority, for a decade. But what if someone on the inside was involved? One of the agents at work on the military data stuck his head into the office.

"We're still working on it, boss. So far there are more than a dozen possibilities."

"Thanks, keep on it. Time is of the essence."

O'Malley looked at his watch again—10:05 a.m. He knew the forensic artist would be at the Professor's home and decided to give him a call. He looked up the cell number on the FBI departmental phone list and keyed in the number.

"Dave? Are you finished with that sketch yet?"

The forensic artist's voice answered. "I'll be there in about twenty minutes."

Thanks," said O'Malley.

He left the desk and walked to the coffee dispenser.

Twenty minutes later the forensic artist walked into his office and set the sketchpad down on the desktop. "That Professor's girl-friend is something," he joked.

"Yeah—definitely one of a kind. Let's have a look at this bastard."

He grabbed the pad and stared at the sketch for a few moments. The forensic artist sat in the chair opposite. "Check those eyes—the professor was really freaked out about them. Says he'll never forget the intensity of the stare."

"They do seem hostile. We need to get this into the system and allow the computer to find a match."

"I have to go," said the artist. He stood, shook O'Malley's hand and left.

It took a minute for O'Malley to scan the sketch into the system and key in the instruction for the search to begin. The faces on the screen rattled off at a record pace and it wasn't long before the match came up. O'Malley checked his watch—11:29 a.m.

He picked up the phone and keyed in Hadley's number.

"Our killer is a Robert Maxwell Coulson. Saw time in Afghanistan and received an honorable discharged, about six months ago. The file shows he suffered from mild symptoms of PTSD. He was involved in a friendly fire incident in which twenty-three Canadian soldiers died. The investigation exonerated him after a lengthy battle—looks like the US Military decided to look after their boy."

The Assistant Director replied. "I don't doubt it. I think we may have found something which could be used to blackmail him with."

"He's currently employed in the Secret Service as a guard dog. We need to notify the Security Chief right away—he could have been assigned to the Presidential detail for St. Louis," said O'Malley.

"Get on it immediately. We don't know if this is the targeted event or not, but let's not take any chances."

*

Bob Coulson ducked around a corner in the corridor and shot up the steps to the third floor where, in accordance with the layout plan the blackmailer gave him, he would find the bathroom. At each level an agent leaned against the balcony and scrutinized the crowd in the auditorium below. He took care not to be noticed as he slipped around the corner of each floor threshold, to race up the stairs to the next level. On the third level he showed his badge to the agent and pointed toward the bathroom. The agent recognized him, nodded and grinned. Inside the room, on the far-side wall a six inch diameter, flanged pipe with a blind on the end, protruded. He opened the designated locker, removed the wrench from its top shelf and went to work on the flange. Another two minutes passed before the flange bolts lay on the floor and he carefully removed the blind. Inside, as per his instructions lay the assassin's rifle, wrapped in plastic. The stock and the barrel needed to be fitted together but it came easily to him. The single sight clipped into position without a sound. One bullet rested in the breech. One more detail needed to be checked. He crept silently to the back wall of the balcony area and opened the narrow window, facing the back of the center's grounds. The entire back of the building had scaffolding attached for construction work on the façade. Satisfied, he crept back into the bathroom and retrieved the rifle.

The agent who watched the auditorium from the center of the balcony did not suspect a thing and didn't even turn around when Bob crept up behind him. Bob removed the service knife from his ankle and thrust it hard, into the back of the man's neck. The hapless agent crumpled at the knees and fell backwards into Bob's waiting arms. He looked over the balcony, across the auditorium, to where President Martin Lewis preached from the podium. No one suspected a thing. The bolt, with its firing pin, moved soundlessly against the back of the shell as he raised the rifle, to fire. The President in full discharge of his speech raised his eyes to see the agents gazing out over each balcony, staring at him. On the third level, a movement caught his eye and a muffled sound floated across the auditorium but before the thought could formulate, the bullet rammed into his forehead.

For two seconds no one moved. The entire audience, including the secret service men, stared in disbelief. The President toppled over backwards and landed on the stage floor and a pandemonium broke out. The two agents on each side of the stage sprang into action and ran hard to the spot where Martin Lewis had fallen. One of them threw himself over the lifeless body while the other scanned the balconies on each floor. He spoke rapidly into his wrist-mic and other agents converged on the stairs from all directions. People screamed and shouted. Many, terrified they may be targeted by the gunman, tried to flee through exit doors and caused so much congestion that the agents struggled to make any headway.

Bob Coulson slipped in through the side exit, which someone had left unlocked for the purpose and made his way up the stairs, to the balconies. No one even saw him enter from outside. He called his colleague on the wrist mic. "Where are you?"

The agent answered. "I'm up here on the third floor balcony—where are you?"

"I'm getting there—just needed to check the exits on the West side."

"The agent, who manned this balcony, is dead. The shooter fired from the third floor," his colleague said.

Bob appeared on the third floor balcony with two other agents, who came up the stairs on the opposite side.

"Jesus—the President's been shot. I think he's dead," said one of the agents.

Bob ran to the half-open window and said, "This is where he must have got in and also made an exit."

The Chief of Security arrived to survey the scene. "Oh my God—we are in ever so much shit. How did this bastard get in?"

*

O'Malley called the Chief of Staff at the White House and explained his position. He supplied all the details on Bob Coulson and how they came to be in possession of the facts, regarding his identity. He stopped short at mentioning the details of the identity sketch's actual origin.

"You need to act on this immediately Sir. Robert Coulson, we understand, had been assigned to protect the First lady—it's possible he might be on the assignment for St. Louis."

The Chief of Staff checked a roster on his computer. "I see he has been selected for that detail. We'll contact the Security Supervisor."

O'Malley checked the time again—11:31 a.m. Ten minutes later the news of the tragedy reached the networks. The assistant director walked into O'Malley's office and sat down. "We were on the right track but acted too late. The President has just been assassinated. There will be an enquiry into when we received the information and how long it took to expe dite, so you had better journal every move you made—from the time of the first murder to your conversation with the chief of staff."

"It could have been done quicker if I'd pushed the Professor to make the sketch last night, instead of this morning but he was in no condition at the conclusion of the experiment."

"I have just spoken to the judge who granted the injunction for use of the memory sweeper. He is not allowing us to say anything about it for the time being. You did what you had to do, Dillon, and we can't change anything now.

"Recognition of Coulson still came via the sweep's sketch—what are we going to say?" asked O'Malley.

"We can use the first sketch, side profile, gathered from the morning Gracie Beauchamp was shot at the Institute. The quality was not good enough to provide the detail required by the recognition software and we can say it took us this long to get a result."

O'Malley shifted uncomfortably in his chair. "It's a half-lie, though—I don't like it."

"I know but the judge is covering his ass and besides, I don't think the world is ready for Wheeler and Pink's invention yet."

∞∞

14

Making an Escape

Bob Coulson knew it would be a matter of time before they tied the murder to him. The initial plan, as set out by the blackmailer provided for a new identity and an escape path to Brazil where he could tap into the Swiss bank account, arranged on his behalf. The provision for escape had worked seamlessly. The scaffold for the facade at the back of the building and the unlocked door, which allowed him access, back into the building, allowed him to mix in with the auditorium's crowd. The time for the rest of the plan to be put to the test, unfolded rapidly with the sudden influx of local law enforcement, which brought a measure of crowd control.

Bob slipped away from his colleague, picked up the small backpack, hidden in a cleaning utilities closet near the exit, and left the building. The backpack contained a denim jacket, a false beard and a wig. A cordon, set up by the local police would not prevent him leaving if he showed his secret service identification. A car should be in a side street two blocks down, outside the initial security area of the conference, to provide him with the means of a quick escape.

The thought that his blackmailer could be lying about this part of the plan, entered his thoughts but he pushed it from his mind. His fear might be well founded. Nothing existed, to tie a blackmailer to the saga and no details could be gleaned, with regards to the originator of the letters. Once the assassination took place the blackmailer could walk away and make no further provision for him—he would be on his own.

People still mingled around inside the auditorium in a state of confusion. A police spokesperson told them to take their seats—no one would be allowed to leave, until vetted by the authorities. They believed the assassin could still be on the premises. Bob walked toward a young policeman on duty at the cordon's perimeter and showed his ID. The man nodded and told hm to walk through. Relieved, he picked up the pace and headed for Melrose Street where he hoped to find the vehicle, a dark, blue sedan, which he would use to get to a small-craft airport, on the outskirts of St. Louis.

According to his final instructions he would find the airline tickets and detailed directions in the glove compartment of the car. On arrival at Melrose Street, no such vehicle could be found and Bob realized the intension of the blackmailer had never been to allow him an escape. This meant the remainder of the plan would not materialize and he was on his own. His instincts had been correct—he would have to bring his own plan into the picture. The train station, a few hundred yards down the road from Melrose Street, would still be accessible for a short period of time and he needed to get there before the police juggernaut increased the cordon, to include all possible escape routes.

They would be expecting the assassin to make an attempt to leave the country but they would never find him where he proposed to go. A safety deposit box at the Post Office in New

York contained all the cash he possessed and he would be able to survive for quite a long while. He needed to leave immediately.

Psychologically, Bob had started to prepare himself for a different lifestyle a short time after the first blackmailer letter arrived in the mail. He saw it as a self-inflicted punishment for his war crime and moral obligation towards some sort of payback. The murder of one bad president did not, in his mind eclipse the heinous crime, of murdering twenty-three soldiers from an allied country. The blackmailer suggested any assassin, with the balls to perform the deed, would be seen as a hero.

Bob, intelligent enough to know this would never produce any form of clemency in a new regime, considered a new administration might not make the search for an assassin a priority, which would give him an opportunity to make a new life for himself. He went along with the blackmailer's story and the provision of a new life, because there appeared to be no alternative. The blackmailer held all the aces— a case of being damned if he did and damned if he didn't.

He pulled into an alleyway to don his disguise and then walked to the train station, to purchase a ticket for New York City.

*

Two Weeks Later

The phone, situated in the kitchen area, woke Lucas from a deep sleep. He grappled with the sheets, to make a quick exit from the warm bed and stumbled over a discarded pillow on the floor.

"Hi Professor. Sorry to wake you so early but I believe we have your man."

It took a few moments for Lucas's mind to clear. "Is that you, Shanks?"

'Indeed, it is."

Lucas looked at the kitchen wall-clock—5:30 a.m. "Which man are you talking about?"

"The bloke whose sketch you gave us."

For a moment Lucas tried to gather his thoughts until the meaning of Shanks's words dawned on him. The murderer. The man who killed Veronica and Gracie—the man who assassinated the President of the United States. The manhunt for Robert Coulson, now in its second week had so far, drawn a blank. The man somehow escaped the tight cordon set up by law enforcement and many thought he might have escaped to a foreign country.

"Where is he, Shanks? Are you sure its him?"

"Positive ID Professor. It took us a little time as the guy was hiding out in the Northside of Manhattan. He stayed away from all the built-up areas and it looks as though he tried to filter in with the local homeless crowd, by wearing a disguise—but one of the people noticed his beard seemed fake. They followed him and bingo, saw him remove it while washing his face one evening."

"You realize this is the guy who assassinated President Lewis, two weeks ago?"

"We read the news, Professor—the papers may be a few days old when we find them but his mugshot is everywhere," said Shanks.

"Give me the details of where he can be found."

Lucas wrote down the information and ended the call. He made a brief search for O'-Malley's personal calling card, keyed in the cellphone number and waited. A moment later, the agent's voice mumbled in his ear.

"Hi, Dillon, Lucas Wheeler—I know its very early in the morning but are you sitting down?"

He related the situation of Shank's discovery and gave the relevant details of how and where the assassin could be found.

*

The Professor's news instilled a hope of justice being served—not so much for the President but for Gracie and Veronica. O'Malley, despite the hour, called his boss and told him the good news.

"Tell no one, Dillon. Take a couple of your best guys and bring him to the holding cells. We need to make absolutely sure its Coulson and not some crackpot, before letting the rest of Law Enforcement know."

"The Media is going to go crazy when they find out, so I'll call in a few of the journalists for a briefing once we've got him in custody," said O'Malley.

"That professor has certainly come through for us. Coulson should know who his black-mailers are, and if not, I think I know how we might get it out of him."

"Are you thinking of asking Wheeler to help us again?" asked O'Malley.

"Its a thought—we can't force him, or the dean of the Institute to comply this time, though."

"You don't think the judge will agree?"

"I doubt it. But maybe you could work on that quirky, pink-headed assistant—I think she's got the hots for you."

O'Malley laughed, then scowled. "Not worth my marriage, thank you, but if the prof isn't keen I'll have a word with her."

Later that morning he gathering four of his ablest agents, instructed them to don casual clothes and drove at high speed, through the traffic to the North of Manhattan, their target area—the corner of Jerome Avenue and East 164th streets, not far from the Yankee Stadium in the Bronx. The professor's homeless contacts guessed Coulson slept somewhere close to the Stadium buildings at nights.

He parked nearby the entrance to the stadium and gave instructions to his men. "I'll wait in the vehicle. Coulson saw me at the Institute on the day he shot Gracie Beauchamp and I don't want to risk him recognizing me. Check all the homeless people you find in the area. Don't come back without him."

The men split into two groups and mingled with the people on the side walk. One of the groups spotted a homeless man lying on the verge, about hundred and fifty yards from the stadium entrance. The man, with hat pulled over his eyes to block out the sun, seemed oblivious to everything around him. A beard jutted out beneath the rim of the hat and the pants he wore looked too new to belong to a tramp. This individual fitted the description given the agents and they couldn't believe their luck at having found a potential suspect so early in their search.

One of the agents walked up onto the grass verge and stood next to the man, who appeared to be asleep and gently lifted the hat off the face. The man's eyes flew open, locked onto those of the agent and he sat upright, in one movement. The revolver appeared in the agent's hands as if by osmosis and pointed at the homeless man's forehead.

"Robert Coulson? You are under arrest for the murders of the Beauchamp sisters and the President of the United States."

Coulson stood to his feet and wiped the sleep from his eyes. "How did you find me?"

"We had a little help from your homeless friends."

The other agent moved behind Coulson and grabbed both arms, bending the wrists behind the small of the back, for the application of handcuffs."

O'Malley saw the men walking in his direction and knew the search to be over. One of the agents gave the thumbs up sign of success, so he called the other group on his cell phone. An Hour later the special agent, with his two groups, arrived back at the FBI headquarters and placed their captive in a holding cell. To the many agents and staff in the building, the homeless man appeared to be another witness to a case, or a source of information, for gang activity. Nobody recognized Robert Coulson, due to the disguise.

O'Malley sat in the Assistant director's office in deep discussion with Don Hadley, his boss. "We have a positive identification with the secret service and military records in confirmation. When are you going to tell the White House and the media?"

"I'll tell them immediately. The Vice President has been champing at the bit for information and I believe he does't think much of the FBI, or CIA , at the moment. This will gain us some favorable Press," answered Hadley.

"Have you heard from the dean of the Institute, regarding the holographic records accumulated from Gracie Beauchamp's memory sweep?"

"Yes, in fact he called this morning to say if we needed them they would be made available. I told him about the judges' reluctance to use the details of the sweep and we had a lead on the assassin from a different source—he was happy about the breakthrough not being used in this respect."

"Did you mention we may need to make use of it again?"

"No—I thought I would leave that to you. It would be better to see what Coulson knows about his blackmailers, first.," said Hadley.

O'Malley stared out of the window for a moment. "It's possible he may not know who they are but maybe the letters containing the instruction will still be available."

"We've searched his apartment from top to bottom—nothing."

"My point is he'll have read them. They will be in his memory and from what we've experienced so far, a sweep will reveal this one vital clue."

"Don't get your hopes up, Dillon. The letters will be cut from available texts in newspapers or magazines—they always are."

"There may be other clues in his past that reflect on the issue of the friendly fire incident he was involved in. There has to be something."

If there is, I'm sure you will find it. I'm going to call the White House."

∞∞

15

Reminiscing a failed Relationship.

The First lady gazed out of the bedroom window at the White House gardens. Boxes of personal affects dotted the floor of the room and a breeze fluttered the velvet curtains, to bring back memories of the fifteen months she and her deceased husband spent in office. Everything about the scene brought back memories and not all of them, good. A sadness filled her heart as she recalled her last moments in the room with him. Her confrontation of his infidelity brought on a strong denial by him and a strained atmosphere filled the final morning of their relationship.

Sheila would never forget the look on her husband's face when she told him she knew about the other woman. His lies and deceit would

always be a painful reminder to her, of what happens to many who achieve fame and fortune—they turn to self-indulgence and ego-tism. It had not always been that way. In his younger days, as an entrepreneur, Martin expressed himself differently and channeled his frustrations into his work. His success at foreign investments, stocks, bonds, property development and many other areas of business, catapulted him into the imagination of the public as a man who knew where he was going. Politics seemed destined to be the ultimate test of his genius, a dream he nurtured for many years, until someone suggested he run for President of the United States.

The Vice President's wife Margaret broke the silence. "A penny for your thoughts?"

"Oh, I was just thinking of Martin's climb to success. It seems only yesterday we entertained the idea of him running for president."

"I see the FBI have just announced that Martin's killer was caught this morning. I'm not surprised he turned out to be someone on the

inside—one of your personal guards. How well did you know this Robert Coulson?"

"I thought I knew him quite well but I never thought he would do something like this. He was always so helpful and polite—I liked him."

"Do you think he acted alone?"

Sheila picked up a framed family photograph and dropped it into one of the boxes. "They don't usually act alone. Martin had many enemies."

"Your husband certainly pissed off a lot of people. It could have been a foreign government, members of the opposition party or even the Press. Didn't he have a few of the left wing journalists fired from their positions, for things they said during his campaign?"

"I don't think about it, Marge. The FBI and CIA are working on it."

"I heard a rumor that the FBI used a unknown memory extraction method on one of the people murdered by your Mister Coulson. The rumor says he murdered the girl because she could identify him. They could actually see into the girl's brain and produce a hologram of the incident—its not official, though."

Sheila stopped and stared at her friend. "They have a means of doing that? I thought someone had identified him after he killed that girl—they had a sketch drawn up."

"That's what the FBI said but I heard that the sketch was not near good enough to make a positive ID."

"How did you come by this information?"

"I am married to the Vice President of the United States. He told me that a judge had granted an injunction to gain the use of this breakthrough technology but did not want to go on record of it being official, because of the collateral damage it could cause. The FBI was searching the girl's memory when someone broke in and shot her—supposedly your Mr. Coulson."

"He's not my Mr. Coulson, Marge, and you shouldn't be listening to these conspiracy theories, anyway. They're just rumors."

"My point is that if this is true, it opens up a whole new way of finding the perpetrators of crime. It means they may eventually find who is behind the plot to murder Martin."

*

O'Malley sat in the dean's office with Lucas Wheeler and Samantha Pink. The holo-graphics of Gracie Beauchamp's terrifying experience at the hand's of the killer, remained as an epic adventure in his mind. The holograms of the events, contained in the holo-files, tended to take the viewer on a virtual journey as they displayed on a special platform designed for the purpose. O'Malley sat transfixed by the show and could not get over how clear the presentation was.

The dean folded his hands on the desktop and scrutinized the special agent. "Why can't you guys use conventional means to find out who's behind the plot?"

O'Malley gave a short laugh. "It's a tall order for our resources. Our assassin was blackmailed into doing the act but he claims he does not know who the blackmailer is. He may not be telling the truth so the only way we can find out is a sweep of his memory. He might be protecting some person for a reason. There may be people in his past who discovered things about him—things he had done."

The dean turned to Lucas and Samantha. "Dillon wants to conduct another experiment with the sweeper. He says it will speed up the process of getting to the bottom of the assassination plot."

Lucas scowled. "I thought it was a one-off thing. I can't say I'm happy about using it for this purpose. It was unfortunate for Gracie Beauchamp to have been collateral damage in the first experiment but with the judge backtracking on his first decision, it may have been a fortuitous situation. Maybe it's just not meant to be."

"Are you still worried about privacy issues?" asked O'Malley.

"I'm worried about what the public are going to say. It may affect the grants we receive from our donors," said the dean.

Lucas raised his chin. "I'm worried it will impact negatively on society. If the process ever becomes commercialized I can see lawyers ordering memory sweeps of innocent people who may get things they don't want revealed, splashed all over the papers."

O'Malley looked thoughtful. "I understand your point. We've been over this ground before but this will be for a good cause. If we don't resolve the issue of the assassination, it will remain like a festering sore in the political fabric of our country. The technology needs some sort of exposure and I can't see there being a better case for its credibility, than this. The assassination is the most prominent crime of the century, so far, and many people are worried that it could happen any time the American people are unhappy with their leadership."

"I gather you will not be seeking an injunction this time?" asked the dean.

"No—I don't think the judge wants the publicity. I think its a moral issue, though. Can we withhold what may be the only means of revealing the source of this evil affair? Would it be fair to the first Lady and her family, to deny them the justice they deserve? Would it be fair to our society, to prevent the surest way of tying this all up?"

"I'm with you, FBI Guy," said Samantha.

O'Malley looked at her with relief. He needed someone to wade in on his side. Samantha leaned forward. "I don't think it's up to us to decide how the invention should be used. Albert Einstein voiced his opinion on the use of atomic energy after some of his research facilitated the ground-breaking manufacture of a bomb, but they used the information anyway."

I hardly think this scenario can be compared to $E=MC^2$, Sam," said Lucas.

"It doesn't matter—I still don't think it's up to us. We can deny the use of it now but once it becomes known we did so, there might be just as many people who'll criticize our decision, anyway."

The Dean narrowed his eyelids. "Sam's right, Lucas. Now that we know the technology works it will be out of our hands. The courts can decide on how it should be morally and legitimately used."

"So we're in agreement then, that the FBI use this for solving the case of the assassination plot?" said Samantha.

Lucas gave her a stern look and she in turn, stuck out her tongue at him. O'Malley and the Dean shook their heads.

There is just one more issue regarding the operation," said Lucas.

The others looked at him expectantly. "I don't want to be the investigator this time."

The dean raised his eyebrows. "I can understand it's a terrible wrench on the mind—are you suggesting Samantha do it?"

The professor chuckled. "No, She already operates on half a brain. I think we need a more investigative mind to step in."

O'Malley smiled. "I thought it would take too long to learn the ropes, Professor?"

Wheeler smiled. "It will take a couple of hours to teach you how to deal with the situation—time we didn't have with the Gracie Beauchamp sweep. I think you will do well with it, Dillon. It's not something I care to do again, personally."

O'Malley leaned back in his chair. "I'll make myself available this afternoon to start the process. I believe, in time, the memory sweep will replace the polygraph test. It'll provide a much greater accuracy and reveal actual circumstances. It will simplify legal decisions."

"You okay with the use of the sweeper for this purpose, Lucas," asked the dean.

He glared at Samantha. "Not really, but I bow to the overwhelming pressure."

She grinned at him. "You're such a pussy."

He smiled benignly. "That's because I work with a tyrant."

O'Malley stood. "I'll be back this afternoon to start the learning process, then we can start the ball rolling. The target will need to be anesthetized and brought to the lab. How long do we need to put him out for?"

"You're not going to get his permission?" asked Lucas.

"I doubt whether he'll comply—would you, if you were in his shoes?"

Lucas screwed up one eye and looked at the ceiling. "I guess not. It raises the question, though—would the holo-file of the sweep be accepted as evidence in a court, if the target has not agreed to it?"

"We're not looking for legal acceptance at this point—just information, which might lead us to the plotter," said O'Malley.

"Tell your anesthetist to make sure Coulson is out for at least one hour while the operation is in progress. We'll conduct the experiment exactly as we did Gracie Beauchamp's."

O'Malley shook hands with the dean and Lucas. He leaned over to take Samantha's hand but she stood and stared into his eyes. "I'm with you, baby—make sure the glock's handy—you just never know who's lurking in the wings."

He blushed as she pecked him on the cheek.

"I'll see you later. I need to clear this with my boss." said O'Malley.

∞∞∞

16

A Meeting of Conspirators

General Leif Hansen opened the file on his laptop and scrutinized the secret service report. After a cursory read he removed a key from his pocket, unlocked one of his desk's drawers and pulled out a cell phone. The encrypted device provided a secure line to certain people of trust. He keyed in a number and waited for a response.

"Your man has finally been caught. The FBI has him locked up in a holding cell."

The recipient answered in a calm voice. "We don't have to worry about a thing. There is nothing to tie him to our group."

"Are you absolutely sure? You heard the rumor about a device the FBI used on one of the girl's he murdered. If they're able to get into Coul son's mind, they'll be able to see his past," said the general.

"It doesn't matter. There is nothing he knows that will incriminate anyone."

"I hope you're right. The FBI will look into his military history and work out certain connections to the friendly-fire incident."

"What of it? They'll find out nothing of importance."

"Only that I was the head of his division and would have had access to all the information regarding his trial," said the general.

"The leak of the information cannot be traced. No one will be able to lay anything at your door—you took care of the only other person who knew about his crime, didn't you?"

"The junior officer who's rape Coulson covered up? I took care of it. There's no one else alive we know of, beside our small group, who knows the whole story."

"Then there's nothing to worry about, is there?"

The general slid a sinewy hand through his military haircut. "I guess not, but I know the FBI won't close the case until they find out who blackmailed Coulson."

"—and we have that base covered, so the case will end up cold, wont it?"

*

The holding cell, situated in the basement of the J. Edgar Hoover building, lacked sufficient lighting and proper ventilation. Bob Coulson felt pangs of claustrophobia and wondered if he would ever see the light of day again. In his mind he thought maybe justice had at last been served. He rued the day when he took that shortcut of military protocol which resulted in the friendly-fire incident. If only it was possible to go back in time but nothing could change that mistake now. The die had been cast the moment he lied to cover up his short-coming. It might have been better had he come clean and accepted the discipline with its consequences—too late now.

He regretted the deaths of the two young women but the blackmailer forced his hand and he acted uncharacteristically, out of fear. He did not regret the death of the President, only being caught for performing the deed. The clang of the cell door brought him back to reality and he looked up to see a man in a white shirt and tie. the dark trousers suggested him to be an FBI agent.

"Mr. Coulson?"

Bob nodded but said nothing.

"I am Special Agent, O'Malley, FBI. I want to talk about your military record."

Bob stared at him and remained silent.

"I see you were involved in a friendly fire incident during your deployment in Afghanistan."

"What of it," asked Bob.

"Was there anything about your actions that day which might have led to the incident?"

"You have access to the record—its all there. I was exonerated of blame."

"I know there are always extenuating situations which lead to this type of incident," said O'Malley."

"Such as what?"

"Maybe not following orders, or perhaps protecting someone who committed a crime," said O'Malley.

"Everything is in the report, O'Malley."

"I'm just wondering if you weren't blackmailed by someone who found that the official record was not quite what it should have been?"

"As I said. The official record carries the true story."

"You do realize how we got on to you, don't you, Coulson?"

"Something to do with the Beauchamp woman and her memory."

"That's correct. We're now able, due to the latest breakthrough in neuroscience, look in on the memories of victims and see what they experienced. We saw Veronica's last entry in her diary, regarding your visit with her. We also saw you kill her sister Gracie and as far as the assassination of the President goes, we know you didn't act alone."

"I'm not saying anything, O'Malley. The President deserved to die—he was a traitor to our country and the most unpopular person ever to hold the office."

O'Malley considered Coulson's outburst. "The two girls didn't deserve it. You have no record of ever voicing your political opinions, Coulson. Why now, suddenly."

"Because I never spoke about it doesn't mean I didn't hold an opinion," said Bob.

"It takes more than an opinion to go out and kill a President, Coulson. Who are you protecting?"

"Forget it, O'Malley," said Bob. He turned his face to the wall to indicate he had nothing further to say on the matter.

"Will you submit to a memory sweep?"

"Not in a million years," said Coulson."

"Then we'll have to do it without your permission."

Bob looked alarmed. "You can't do that—its a violation of my sovereign rights."

"You lost all your sovereign rights when you murdered those two girls and the President."

"I won't submit to any sort of testing."

While you're still in the custody of the FBI you'll have no choice."

"You won't get anything."

"We'll see," said O'Malley. He turned, walked out and locked the cell door behind him.

*

Lucas and Samantha sat at the lab bench with arms touching and heads close together, both lost in concentration. Their focus of attention lay in the diagrams on a piece of paper. Every now and then Samantha would type instructions into a computer program and both would reflect on the results, visible on the monitor.

Lucas made a quick scribble in the margin of the diagram. "So we can safely say that the effects of glial cleanup operations would not harm the avatar providing the correct pace is maintained throughout the investigation?"

"This will be difficult because the avatar can't maintain this pace and investigate at the same time," answered Samantha.

"We didn't have glial problems with Gracie Beauchamp due to the low state of her system, but this Coulson guy will be a different story."

"The most important thing for O'Malley to know is what to tell Echo to do in the event of glial pruning taking place, while the avatar is moving at an investigative pace."

"So let's discuss his options," said Samantha.

Lucas thought through what he saw as options. "If it gets really dangerous Echo can increase the speed of the avatar, however, the memory being investigated will be lost and there can be no turning back. What if we program a release of a higher voltage of conductivity which might reform the glia?"

Samantha look dubious. "A higher conductivity range might cut through the myelin formation but it may also be dangerous for the avatar's directional path."

"This is true but Echo can scan the developing pathways to see if the avatar can find a new direction."

"Except that the memory will still be lost," complained Samantha.

The dean's voice intervened in their intense discussion, drawing them both back to the real world.

"Your student has arrived. Are you ready to brief him?"

"I think we have enough to begin with. We don't wan't to overwhelm the poor FBI guy," said Samantha.

"Good. I'll bring him through," said the dean.

He left and moments later returned with O'Malley in tow.

The FBI agent looked tense and alert as he sat in the chair offered him.

"I'm ready to begin. Do I need to take notes?"

"It would be advisable," said Lucas.

Samantha picked up a pen and a note pad from the desk. "Here we are my pet. They teach you to write in FBI school?"

"Not really but I know how to draw pictures," said O'Malley. They all laughed and the tenseness seeped out of O'Malley's soul.

"I'll be in my office if you need me," said the dean.
Samantha chuckled. "We need you like a hole in the head, Deansy."

To O'Malley's chagrin she sat down on his lap, placed her arms around the agent's neck and planted a kiss on his forehead.

He turned red. "Is this how you treat all your student's, Sam?"

She smiled. "Only the one's I fancy."

Lucas brought things to order. "Let's start with exactly what you are in for. Firstly, understand that the process will play havoc with your nervous system. With the left and right brain functions separated, but still in contact through the quantum process of entanglement, it will give you a sensation of floating out in space."

"How do the two perspectives interface over the distance?" asked O'Malley.

"There is instantaneous interfacing, however, the brain's logic and deductive powers will be at variance with each other. I won't say anything more about this aspect because there is nothing you can do to prevent the feeling it gives you."

"Sounds comforting," said O'Malley.

"The next thing you need to be prepared for is the presence of Echo, our command control computer program. Echo is extremely capable and smart but she needs some direction when the unexpected happens."

"The unexpected?" asked O'Malley.

"We are dealing with a brain that's healthy and not struggling to keep the body alive. The target is also a violent man who thinks in terms of destructive actions to resolve issues—how this will effect the presence of an investigator is something which we know very little about."

"Are you saying Coulson can direct any of his internal nervous system's defenses to attack the avatar?"

"We don't know, Dillon. This is the part of the process that scares me. A lot of our body's function is affected by our thought processes—usually in a negative way. If you think negatively you release certain hormones and endorphins that can alter the biology of your body."

Samantha, back in her chair, jumped into the conversation. "We have these nasties called the Glial cells which are there to protect the function of the neurons and, which we believe, prune away unwanted material. They propagate a fatty substance called myelin which forms around the axons during the formation of the nervous system and act as an insulation."

Lucas cut her off and continued. "There is also a type of glial cell called microglia, which monitors synaptic transmissions. These cells can rewire the neuronal connections which propagate the signals and thus prevent the avatar from jumping from cell to cell."

"Is this something to be worried about?" asked O'Malley.

"Only when you are trying to hang around in a memory, sweetie," said Samantha.

"I'm sure I'll be in good hands with Echo at the helm."

"She is programmed to ask you what you want to do in tough situations. If you are at a loss then you must tell her to act on the closest solution—she will always seek the safest way out, even if that means to abort the mission."

∞∞

17

Grief Counseling

Janet and Dillon O'Malley sat on the settee in the FBI psychologist's office and stared out of the window. The psychologist, caught up in another case called her secretary to let the couple know she would be up in a few minutes and to apologize for the wait.

O'Malley recalled their last visit almost eighteen months ago. The conversation got bogged down in his pretentious stoicism and Janet's insistence that they would find a way to work through their pain, together. The psychologist emphatically told them it would take a long time, to get through the stages of grief and it would not be a good thing to stop counseling because they didn't feel it worked for them. Janet knew her attitude, at the time, prevented her moving on to more productive thinking and O'Malley's indifference toward counselors, didn't help him to resolve anything.

The previous night's argument, however, caused warning bells to go off in his mind and he suggested they resume the sessions, a suggestion to which she responded positively. The door opened and the psychologist walked in.

"I'm so glad you two have decided to try counseling again. I felt our last session kind of got bogged down," she said.

"We've realized, that without help our marriage will continue to suffer—it has just not been possible to move on," said Janet.

"Let's go over the details of Fallon's death and then I want both of you to tell me what you think is preventing your from moving on. I know it will be painful to dredge up the facts again but it will help me to gage your latest perspectives."

Janet opened up first. "On the fateful evening of her death, Dillon and I were watching TV. It was the night of the school prom. We aren't sure why Fallon ended up with the group of teenagers in a car but it is assumed they left the party to go somewhere. The driver of the car, a brother of a prom student, had been drinking before the event and others say he bragged about a street race, which he would be taking part in later that evening."

O'Malley picked up the story. "We assume they were on their way to this street racing venue, when the accident happened. A drunk driver jumped a red light and their car was hit by the other vehicle, traveling at high speed. The driver of the other vehicle was never apprehended."

"How were you informed?" asked the psychologist.

"We received a call at 9:21 p.m. that evening. The caller, a member of the local police precinct, told us there had been an accident and Fallon, along with two other children, had succumbed to their injuries. They were DOA at the hospital," said Janet.

"How did you feel at that moment?"

Janet hesitated. "My world crashed."

The psychologist turned to look at O'Malley. "Dillon?"

O'Malley's mind could not think how to put his feelings into words and for a moment he stared at her. The old notion regarding the inefficacy of the questions from previous sessions returned—anger and hopelessness started to to rise within him again. He looked at the ceiling and tried to compose himself. The inevitableness of the frustration felt, when asked about the disaster, surfaced and he fought hard to overcome it. The first words sounded strangulated. O'Malley stopped in mid-sentence to regain composure.

"I could not believe what was happening to us—it didn't seem real," he said.

The psychologist nodded and turned to Janet. "Jan?"

Janet looked at O'Malley and the tears welled up in her eyes. "I'm sorry—this never seems to get easier. I felt as though my life had been ripped away from me. We rushed to the hospital but she was already dead—I never got the chance to say goodbye to my baby. Something died inside me the moment I saw her blood-streaked face."

O'Malley reached over to place a reassuring hand on his wife's shoulder. For a moment she buried her face in shaky hands and made a concerted effort to regain control of her emotions.

The psychologist reached over with a tissue and Janet gratefully took it. "Tell me how you feel it compacted your relationship with each other?"

Janet straightened up and dabbed at her eyes with the tissue. "We did our best to comfort each other but Dillon felt such guilt and I felt a terrible anger toward life. He was placed on immediate stress leave which did nothing to help the way he felt. We couldn't sleep at night and for days I walked around like a Zombie."

"What happened with your son, Steven?"

"Steven was only twelve and nothing appeared real to him. He walked around in complete denial and it seemed he got on with his life, however, kids tend to internalize these things," said O'Malley.

"Why did you feel guilty, Dillon?" asked the psychologist.

O'Malley scrutinized his hands and took several moments to answer the question. "I feel guilty because as a father, I didn't prepare Fallon adequately enough for that evening."

"What do you mean?"

Again, O'Malley hesitated. The logistics of this question bothered him and to give the answer a fair chance at making sense, it needed to be framed carefully.

"Fallon was always so level headed. She never seemed to not know when something was wrong—she possessed a maturity beyond her years. I felt I was playing the role of mr. popular, when I allowed her to figure out what was right, on her own. I guess I didn't figure on hormones taking over."

"Are you saying you should have foreseen the possibility of young people cutting lose at a party?"

"I should have known there was the potential for it and given her instructions to remain at the prom—I'm sure she would have listened to me."

"In my experience, Dillon, we can never anticipate what a teenager will do regarding parental instruction when faced with the excitement of danger, and under hormonal influences."

"I believe she would have listened to me. It would have at least given her the opportunity to think about her decision," said O'Malley.

"I hear you. But as you said, she was level-headed for her age and always seemed to know when something appeared wrong. The decision was still hers to make."

O'Malley didn't say anything.

"Do you blame each other?" asked the psychologist.

Janet and O'Malley looked at each other for a brief moment.

"I think blame is a strong word. We may feel, individually as parents, we failed Fallon in different ways," said Janet.

"Dillon?"

He stared out of the window and thought about his answer. "I agree with Jan—blame is a strong word. I think, though, we saw some discipline issues differently. I feel Janet would have liked me to have been stricter with certain things, in what Fallon was exposed to."

The psychologist leaned forward. "Are you saying Janet blames you for not being strict enough, Dillon?"

"As I said, blame is perhaps a strong word."

"Janet?"

The muscles around Janet's mouth tightened. "While its true Dillon could have tightened up on discipline I don't blame him for anything."

It sounds awfully like blame to me, honey," said O'Malley.

∞∞

18

Bob Coulson's Memory

They chose a Sunday to conduct the sweep of Bob Coulson's memory. No one would be on campus that day and but for the dean, Samantha and Lucas, the place was empty. The FBI took no chances with the security. A squad of FBI police occupied every possible entrance and exit of the building. Four men stood guard outside the lab door and two more at each end of the corridor.

"I feel I'm in bloody Fort Knox?" said Samantha.

"Better safe than sorry. We won't forget last time very easily," said O'Malley.

"I thought the target would be anesthetized?" asked the dean.

"It's a strange thing. Initially, when I first interviewed him, he was adamant he would not submit to testing. Early this morning, I brought the anesthetist with me to his cell, to prepare for the event and he told me it would not be necessary for us to put him out."

"How come the change of heart?" asked Lucas.

"I don't really know. I figure he knew we would do the sweep anyway—I told him as much. Maybe, he thinks he can more actively oppose the avatar mentally, if he is awake."

Lucas looked grim. "This is the part which we know very little about. You'll have to beware of "dimming."

"What's that?" asked O'Malley.

"It's the potential the mind possesses, to dim the memory of a particular event, by shear willpower. This is all theory, of course, but a valid argument. We are not even aware of how it might play out."

"I guess I'll find out. Would it be any better if we did put him out?" asked O'Malley.

"Not sure—he's already predisposed to the event," said the dean.

Lucas looked thoughtful. "I guess we could do it again if the memories are too badly dimmed for the record. On the second try we could anesthetize him. The brain is a marvel at rerouting, reconstructing and fabricating the means to protect itself. The exercise should be an excellent test of what we can expect."

"Initially, I was elated he decided to agree to us doing the sweep. It poses less of a legal argument for the violation of rights principle, but now I'm not so sure." said O'Malley.

Bob Coulson sat in the chair beneath the harness, shackled at the wrists and ankles. No expression displayed over his calm features and his eyes reflected no emotion of any sort. Samantha busied herself in the setup of the system while the dean, O'Malley and the professor engaged in conversation. O'Malley supplied Samantha with a flash drive of his FBI file for Echo's purposes, so she would know all about him, which Samantha with her usual adamant charm, said would be necessary for the computer to respond to his style of investigation.

O'Malley hoped nothing of his private life would figure in Echo's summation of his abilities and tendencies. The file contained information regarding the death of his daughter and the counseling sessions to date. He didn't think Samantha would bother to look through the file after she plugged it into a USB port and his secrets would remain at Echo's disposal. When the sweep successfully concluded he would ask for the return of the drive, leaving no record of his file on the computer's system.

Samantha smiled at him. "You can take your seat now, honey. Let Aunty Sam tuck you in and prepare you for your epic journey."

O'Malley sat in the investigator's chair like an obedient puppy and allowed her to smooth his hair before the application of the harness. She tightened the clamp at the back of his head and planted a kiss on his forehead. He enjoyed the attention and gave her a wry smile. "Will I feel any pain?"

"Not if I can help it, ducky."

The smile departed as she moved over to Bob Coulson and stared into his eyes. "I can't say the same for you, you bastard."

The dean raised his eyebrows and Lucas smiled. "You should give him the full force of the accelerator's power, Sam," said the professor.

"I would love to cut his balls off," she said.

Coulson made no comment and the expression on his face did not change.

Samantha looked at Lucas. "We're ready, my king."

"Set Echo in motion, woman—what're you waiting for?"

She looked over at Coulson, gave one of her maniacal laughs and turned on the particle accelerator. The overhead screen lit up as her fingers flew over the keyboard and O'Malley said his prayers. The dean took a seat while Lucas stood beside her and checked out the

telemetry of signals flashing on and off as the avatar came to life.

The information-bearing particles came up to operational speed and zoomed around the outer circuit under the guidance of Echo, ready to pick up the consciousness of O'Malley's right brain hemisphere. The special Agent braced himself for what he knew would be the most traumatic, but epic trip, of his lifetime.

*

General Leif Hansen perused the file on his laptop with a nervous energy. He needed to rekindle his understanding regarding the friendly fire incident, which took place in Afghanistan, almost three years prior. It seemed a long time ago. Nothing could be left to chance and the reopening of the case, the last thing anyone wanted, must not happen. He read through the investigation officer's report three times and reflected on his own testimony. The Canadians could never gain access to the real truth. Twenty-three soldiers dead—the real reason covered up by his own inclusion of a bogus report on the radio communications of that particular morning.

Nothing could be changed now. As long as the report did not come under further scrutiny he would be safe—they would all be safe. The assassination had not been his brainchild but he agreed with the need to remove President Lewis. The others involved all agreed it a necessary action to prevent the dumping of nuclear material on the open market by Russia and a trade revolt by many of the U.S. trading partners. America would be facing a formidable crisis with NATO if Lewis continued with his outlandish foreign policies. They had been on the verge of another world war, but with the removal of the current president from office, things started to look better for peace. The Vice President, a sympathizer but not involved in the assassination plot, would steer the process toward better pastures.

He pulled up another file under the name of Second Lieutenant, John Alistair Ramsey—deceased. The cause of death, listed as an automobile accident while on furlough, displayed the headshot of the young officer whom Coul

son had blackmailed into making a false report, in regards to the friendly fire incident. The report of the second lieutenant's rape of a young afghani girl never saw the light of day because it had been taken care of—nothing seemed out of the ordinary about the official reports. Ramsay was the only other person who could have shed light on the incident.

He called his contact at the FBI. "What more can you tell me about the case on Coulson?"

The contact cleared his throat. "They took him to the Neuro-Technical Institute this morning, to conduct a search of his memory. Special Agent O'Malley is leading the investigation but we don't have anything to worry about—I have ordered it to be shut down. "

*

O'Malley felt a warm sensation start in the back of his head, accompanied by a buzzing sound, which became louder until it reached an almost unbearable pitch. Then with a sudden bang everything became dark and silent. A moment later an indigo hue lit up his immediate surroundings and he gained the impression of skimming along the top of a monstrous wave like a windsurfer, with all the accompanying elements of wind and spray. Flashes of brilliant, white effervescence boiled around him—the windsurf board seemed to lift under his feet, to transport him into a void of muted sounds and vibrant colors. It left him breath-less with wonder.

The forward momentum slowed with a sudden lurch and the indigo hue returned to illuminate the scene around him, of which he could make no immediate sense. The forward motion smoothed out with an occasional jump and it felt as though he was riding on the edge of a light beam, in a large vacuum of space. He understood the sights that came to him were not seen with the physical eye—but appeared to command the same sense of perception—the eye of the soul.

"Hello, Dillon."

The feminine voice sounded sexy, with a sultry sensuality and at the same time the in-flections expressed a silky undertone of elo-quence.

"Hi, Echo—I see you've found me."

"I'm sure we're going to be good friends, sweetie."

"You sound just like Samantha."

"In certain ways I am Sam—she created me."

"So I'm told and yet, around me, I see every color, but pink."

"I'm pink at heart, my king, but enough about me—I find your profile very interesting."

"I'm no one special, Echo. If you look past the veneer you'll see a very ordinary person."

"Is that how you see yourself, Dillon?"

O'Malley gave a mental shrug. "Not just ordinary but also fallible."

"You could work on your insecurities. I perceive you've been deeply affected by the death of your daughter, Fallon."

O'Malley felt a sudden twinge of anger. he hadn't come on the journey to be psychoanalyzed. "Let's drop the psychology lesson, Echo. We've a job to do, so please get on with explanations—I have lot's of questions."

"Certainly, o'great one. What would you like to know?"

To start with, I'm having difficulty seeing my immediate surroundings. Where are we, exactly?"

"Don't be perturbed by what you see, Dillon. Remember you are totally right-brained at the moment—everything you look at will be reduced to the detail of its makeup. We are in the cerebral cortex of Mr. Coulson's brain and making good headway toward the targeted banks of his memory."

"Everything is of an indigo hue—what does this mean?"

"The hue is an artificially induced color for any area that is not a memory."

"Will this change?"

"The color will change when we reach the areas where memories are being stored. Within these areas, the age of each memory will follow the colors of the electromagnetic spectrum. As the memories become more recent, the wave length gets shorter and the colors will change through red to violet."

"In what part of the brain structure are we?"

"We are within the cytoskeleton of the brain and traveling through a passage of neurons toward the areas where the memories are stored. Each neuron is made up of dendrites, a soma or cell, and axons, which transmit the messages from cell to cell. Chiefly, we locate the axon exiting each cell and allow it to transmit us through to the next soma. Sometimes we need to enter a dendrite, because it's the shorter route."

"Why do I feel a lurch and surge, every so often?"

"It happens when the avatar breaches a synapse between an axon and a dendrite."

"Professor Wheeler mentioned there are some nasty cells which hang around to protect the brain—something starting with a 'g'?"

"They are called glial cells, my captain."

"When can we expect an attack by these monsters?"

"Only once we enter the areas of memories, sweetie. Relax, we're not there yet."

The avatar moved along with the smoothness of a conveyor and O'Malley, out of questions for the present, looked around him in wonder. The indigo hue continued to illuminate the walls of the axon as they moved along in silence. He could see vague structures and at times, they entered cavernous areas, which he understood to be the avatar passing through a cell. Without warning, a sudden violent jerk started and the avatar leaped upward, then jinked from left to right. The indigo hue began to transcend into a deep red and it felt as though something banged up against the outside shell of particle grouping.

"What's happening, Echo?"

"Hold onto your FBI credentials, Special Agent—we're crossing a synaptic cleft where we are going to be vulnerable to the attack from glial cells. I believe we are entering the long term memory area and a Glial cell has spotted us."

∞∞

19

Glial Cells

Samantha ran a hand through her pink, spiky hair. The dean, Lucas and the assistant director of the FBI who had arrived unannounced, stood around the computer console, their eyes glued to the screen above.

"They have entered an area of memory. The avatar is jerking about wildly—I think we may have a bit of trouble on our hands," said Samantha.

No specifics appeared on the screen other than a dot of white light, which jiggled about within the confines of a corridor.

"I believe the glial cells are starting their defense of the memory banks," said Lucas.

"What do these glial cells do, Professor?" asked Hadley.

"Glials are the janitors of the memory bank's corridors and arborists of the memory trees. They clean away any used up neurotransmitters and also prune the branches of the trees, or the memories which have not properly formed," answered Lucas.

"Are they a danger?"

"Very dangerous. We haven't yet experienced the full onslaught of their defenses. Gracie Beauchamp's system was at its lowest, primarily because she was dying and the glial cells of her brain couldn't put up any defense at all," said the dean.

"What can the avatar do to protect itself?" asked Hadley.

"Move out of the glial cell's way. Echo can also release the magnetic field contained within the information-bearing particles, to hinder the cell's pruning abilities. As a final resort, should all else fail, she can abort the sweep and get out."

Samantha leaned forward to scrutinize the image on the screen. "The avatar has almost

come to a standstill. Let me check on what Echo's thoughts are."

Her fingers flew over the keyboard in rapid patterns of type, keying in instructions. On the top left of the screen a message appeared:

Hold your horses, Sam—as you can see, I'm busy.

Samantha shot a quick glance at Lucas. He responded in typical fashion. "Don't look at me, sweetheart. She's your creation and she's just doing what you would do in the circumstance."

Samantha scowled and stuck out her tongue. "Thank you so much for your support, dick-head."

"You're welcome, moron," retorted Lucas.

Hadley, with a half-smile looked inquiringly at the dean, who shrugged and averted his gaze to the ceiling.

"I don't like this—the avatar is hardly moving and if it's a glial cell on the attack, Echo should know better. They need to move past it with all speed," said Samantha.

As if Echo heard her words the avatar lurched forward and began to pick up speed. Within a minute it perambulated along as before.

"Whatever it was they seem to have overcome it," said the dean.

Lucas looked over at the investigator's chair where O'Malley sat with his eyes closed. The perspiration started to bubble up on O'Malley's brow and upper lip—his head slumped forward.
"Is he okay?" asked Hadley.

Samantha got up out of her chair and approached O'Malley. She placed her hand on the side of his throat and ran her other hand through his dark, bushy hair.

"He's fine. The left brain is adjusting to having its counterpart out galavanting with the avatar and is getting used to the communication by entanglement."

Hadley looked puzzled. "What do you mean by entanglement?"

"The left brain consciousness is in immediate contact with the right brain consciousness, but at a distance. The right brain has a temporary residence in the avatar and maintains contact by means of a super-position, or the entanglement of the dual setup's particle activity, associated with a protein called tubulin."

"I remember a bit about that from high school quantum physics—I've always thought it was a load of bull." said Hadley.

Samantha shot him a cold glare. "Today, it's pure and acceptable science." She didn't like Hadley. He possessed a condescending attitude.

"Whatever," he said.

She returned to the console and decided to ignore the FBI assistant director.

"I have to go—but I'll expect a full report of what you discover here today," said Hadley.

Lucas smiled, adding his own brand of condescension. "I'm sure Special Agent O'Malley will provide you with whatever you wish to know—we are far too busy to make out official reports for the FBI."

Hadley glared at him, turned and walked out of the lab.

"Supercilious prick. Thinks he owns the joint." said Samantha.

The dean cocked his head to one side."Now, now, Sam. It won't do for you to antagonize the FBI."

Samantha didn't look up from the keyboard. "I don't give a fig about, Hadley. His nothing but a pompous, condescending idiot."

Lucas raised his eyebrows. "Well said, half-brain."

"You're welcome, asshole."

The dean glanced at Lucas and made for the door. "I'm getting out of here. let me know when things cool down a bit."

The overhead screen displayed a type of schematic, along which the avatar conducted its investigation of the memory trees. "Progress appears to have slowed down and they are crossing over another synaptic cleft." said Samantha.

Lucas stared at the blip of white light. "Assuming it came across a glial cell, I hope the avatar has not sustained any damage. It should be making better progress than this."

"Echo must be heavily occupied with whatever's happening—still no message from her," said Samantha.

*

O'Malley peered ahead through the reddish haze of his surroundings and braced himself. He could see a massive balloon-like structure directly in their path and it possessed tentacles like an octopus, stretched out in all directions. Each tentacle-arm flailed around in an effort to grab onto whatever foreign object might be perceived as a threat. A dark, gray color distinguished it from the occasional balls of positive ly charged potassium and sodium ions, which enhanced the propagation of the electrical signals within the axon.

"What the hell is that thing?" asked O'Malley. The nervous quiver in his voice revealed the sudden fear he felt regarding his safety.

"That, my captain, is a glial cell," answered Echo.

"It's huge—how are we going to get around it?"

"We'll attempt to stun it with a blast of radiation. I am initiating the action as we speak."

O'Malley became alarmed. "Will this not be dangerous for the target? Where does this radiation come from?"

"To answer your questions, o' great one— the blast is on such a minuscule scale it makes any effect on the human body, practically negligible. The source of radiation is tied up in the weak nuclear force of the particles which make up the avatar. I am able to release this force under certain circumstances."

"What if it doesn't work?" asked O'Malley.

"Oh yea of little faith. If it doesn't work we have two options, sweetie—find something that works or abort."

"Thanks for the encouraging heads up, Echo. This is when I wish I had my Glock revolver."

"Unfortunately, Glocks do not come in nano sizes, my love."

The Glial cell moved ominously toward their position and its frame filled the entire corridor of the axon. The swinging tentacles reach out to latch onto the avatar and as it did, O'Malley perceived a pressure being brought to bear on the cage-like structure. The avatar lurched sideways as the cell made contact and tightened its tentacled grip. A sudden flash of white light illuminated everything and the avatar started a spasm of movement as if in a convulsion. O'Malley felt as though his life would be ripped from him at any moment. More light flashes followed, which caused a vibration to course through the entire avatar and left him in fear of his very existence.

"Shouldn't we abort, Echo?" cried O'Malley.

"Not yet, my scared little FBI guy. I believe we can win this one."

The convulsing continued and the flashes of light became even more intense as Echo applied greater magnitudes of radiation into the outer shell of the glial cell. When O'Malley thought everything would fail it became quiet and the glial released its hold. The tentacles withdrew and the cell floated away, as though unconscious. The avatar surged ahead with a sudden jerk and squeezed past the body of the cell.

"Well done, Echo. I believe we won the battle," said O'Malley. He felt an intense relief to be on the move again.

"You're welcome, my captain. I maxed out on the amount of radiation the particles could muster and had the battle continued for a few more seconds, we might have been done for."

"That's comforting to know. Let's hope we don't meet any more of them—particularly one that size."

Echo went silent for a period and then made a startling revelation. "I think we might have sustained some damage to some of the avatar's particles, due to the out-source of nuclear energy."

O'Malley sensed a sudden chill in his virtual atmosphere. "What do mean? How will it affect us?"

"We've lost some of the immanent energy which causes our physical progress through the neuro-conduits—it will slow us down, some."

"How far are we from the area of memory we're looking for?" asked O'Malley.

"We have some distance to cover. I suggest you take a rest, o' great one. I'll let you know what transpires."

"Thanks Echo—the ships in your capable hands."

∞∞

20

Back to the Conspirators

The chairman of the Joint Chiefs sat at his desk and leaned forward to rest his chin in the palm of his hand, while he stared at the monitor. Opposite him sat general Leif Hansen, commandant of the U.S. Marine Corps and next to him, sat the director of the FBI.

"Are you sure there's nothing to tie us to Coulson?" He asked.

"Absolutely sure. The blackmail letters were cut from old magazines and pasted onto blank sheets of paper, which Coulson told the FBI, he destroyed," said Hansen.

"Destroying the evidence won't mean a thing if this new-fangled memory sweeper can do what the experts boast."

"It still wont lead anyone to us," said Hansen.

"What magazines were used?"

"Old DIY magazines I kept in the Attic. I've destroyed all of them."

"Good—we can't afford to leave any evidence of our involvement, Leif."

The chairman inspected his finger nails. "I made a bit of a thing, to the assistant director, about releasing Coulson's records but withholding them would only have created suspicion. I think we all knew this day would come. Provided Coulson doesn't know who his blackmailers are, we're safe. O'Malley and this team, who run this new innovation, cannot be allowed to connect the dots. Do I make myself clear?"

Hansen glanced over at the FBI director."We will keep abreast of things, I promise."

*

"Finally, a message from Echo," said Samantha.

Lucas turned from his work at the lab's main table and gave her an enquiring look. "What was the problem."

"More like, what 'is' the problem. A glial cell attacked and nearly destroyed them."

"Any damage?" asked Lucas.

"Apparently. Their speed has been affected due to loss of energy from the avatar's particles. She says they were banged about a bit but eventually managed to stun the cell and move past it."

"Good—at least we know radiation bombardment works. Is O'Malley okay?"

"He's shaken, but fine. They're moving toward the target area of memory, but with lesser momentum."

"Once in the long-term memory area there will be less glial activity and the avatar should have enough assumed energy from the neurotransmitters to make the entire journey."

A message blinked on off, on the lefthand, top area of the screen. "URGENT." Samantha returned her attention to the monitor. "I am getting an urgent message from Echo. They've accessed the first of the target memories and Coulson is not cooperating."

Lucas moved to the console and squinted up at the monitor. "He's dimming the images by concentrating all his mental acuities on recalling another memory."

"I'm going to see if I can distract him," said Samantha.

She got up and walked to Coulson's position. He didn't blink, nor change the direction of his stare, to focus on her. She raised her hand and slapped him as hard as she could. "I've been wanting to do that ever sense you were brought in here, you bastard."

Coulson shook his head and glared at her, his focus of attention disrupted. She held his eyes for about ten seconds before he averted his gaze back to the opposite wall. A hint of a smile played on the corners of his mouth.

A cough at the lab door caught their attention. The dean leaned against the door jamb. "I have just had a call from Hadley, the assistant director. He has been told by his boss to shut down the Coulson memory sweep operation."

Samantha looked alarmed. "Shut it down? We can't just shut it down—we can recall the avatar and Echo will abort the process otherwise Dillon's mental stability could be endangered."

The dean looked passively at her. "I told him as much but he says to shut it down anyway."

Lucas glanced at the dean. "The director of the FBI is only finding out about this now?"

"I thought Hadley was the director," said Samantha.

"He's the assistant director. Apparently, his boss has been out of town and when the director found out about the memory sweep operation he threw all his toys out of the cot."

"Dillon won't be happy about this," said Lucas.

"I said I would start the shutdown process," said the dean.

"Hadley and his boss are colossal turds. They are virtually at the point of being able to begin the investigation of memories—Dillon might see something that will help the FBI solve the conspiracy," said Samantha.

"For once I agree with you, Sam. I wasn't happy to use the sweeper this way but all in all, it's proved the technology is sound."

"And we caught Coulson," said the dean.

"I bet Hadley will come to make sure we shut it down." said Samantha.

They looked at O'Malley's passive face. The eyes still closed, twitched every now and then, to reveal reactions from activity in the left side of his brain. Coulson sat rigidly upright with his wrists manacled to the arms of the chair and eyes wide open. He stared at one spot on the far wall and but for the odd blink, did not alter his gaze.

"You'd better relay the message to Echo. She can start the abort process immediately—perhaps it's for the best," said Lucas.

Samantha typed in several commands and waited. Echo's answer came back with immediate effect. *"Instruction to abort acknowledged."*

*

O'Malley observed the subtle change in background color, from deep red through shades of crimson, which increased in intensity.

*"We have entered the more recent memory area,"*said Echo.

"I see the changes in background color. When will we begin to see the actual detail of the memories?"

"I am slowing the avatar down which will bring the memories into focus, my captain."

O'Malley felt the change of pace, and true to Echo's words, images began to materialize all around the avatar.

He gaped wide eyed at the apparitions. "This is wonderful—it's like being in the center of a hologram."

"You need to make a commentary for the record, sweetie."

O'Malley composed himself. "I'm creeping along with a group of soldiers and we're approaching some burned out vehicle chassis on the opposite side of the road. The radio, on the back of a soldier next to me is crackling to life —it appears we are receiving a message."

"Can you hear the words, Dillon?"

O'Malley strained to hear the words of the message through the static. "I can't hear it adequately...oh—wait, the radio operator is turning to tell me something."

He listened intently for a few seconds and then confirmed what had been said. "We are being told that a group of Canadian soldiers is operating in the area. The intelligence report is giving us coordinates for their position and we are being told not to fire on anyone—even if we are fired upon—until the contact is verified to be the enemy."

"From whose point of view are you observing, my captain?"

"I must be seeing and hearing the ensuing detail through the eyes of Coulson. He appears to be in command of this group."

O'Malley could not believe how real his surroundings appeared. Foreign sounds and smells invaded his senses and with one swift movement he found himself at ground level, at the noise of rapid assault, rifle fire.

"I'm being shot at," he cried. The sudden fear in his voice became palpable. He could see his own hand indicating something to the other soldiers.

The soldier with the radio shouted at him but he shook his head and indicated again. A fire-fight broke out all around them. His group took rifle fire but no one was hit. He beckoned to a man behind him, carrying an RPG.

"Hit them where it hurts," he screamed.

The soldier with the RPG pointed the weapon in the direction from which the rogue fire came and pulled the trigger. He reloaded and fired again.

O'Malley flinched. "I can hear explosions happening across the road. And oh...suddenly all is quiet."

The illumination around his scene started to darken without warning. The images of the soldiers seemed to melt into obscurity and he struggled to make out what they were doing.

"I can't see much, Echo. What's happening?"

"Your target is trying to dim the images deliberately. Coulson has picked up that he is vividly reliving the friendly-fire incident and is doing his best to obscure the images by calling on contrary memories. He knows the avatar must have breached those scenes. He is moving his mental energy to another time and place."

O'Malley knew Echo told the truth. He could see a new image, in the form of a blur, attempting to supplant the scene of the firefight. He could hear shrill voices from another unknown scene, which overshadowed the firefight spectacle. The overdubbed scene gained ascendency and the war memory began to diminish.

"I see a blurry court scene and a panel of high-ranking officers. Another officer, I assume to be the prosecutor is sitting on one side. Everyone is trying to talk at once and the central figure on the panel of judges, is banging a gavel on the desktop. Beneath this is the original scene of the fire-fight and I can't see what the outcome of either memory is."

"I will have to ask Sam to distract the target, somehow."

"Or we move on to another memory," said O'Malley.

"The target will still be retained in the same frame of mind as to his thoughts, so it won't help to move on. I am sending a message as we speak."

A few moments later the blurry scene changed to focus more on the fire-fight again and O'Malley could see the shapes of the soldiers with more clarity. Ten seconds later, however, the images started to blur again.

"Whatever she did worked for a few seconds but its all blurry again," he said.

Echo remained silent for several moments while O'Malley tried to make sense of the picture he saw. Then she made a declaration.

"I am getting a message to abort the sweep."

O'Malley did a double take. "From who?"

"Sam is saying that Don Hadley's boss has ordered him to shut the sweep down immediately."

"The director must be back from his trip. I don't understand why he would do that," spluttered O'Malley.

"It doesn't make any sense, Dillon—but I guess we will have to comply."

"No way are we going to comply with that order—not until I see Coulson's more recent memories. Tell Sam we need a little more time and she needs to find a way to neutralize Coulson's mental abilities."

"Will you not be jeopardizing her career, my king?"

O'Malley went silent for a few moments. "I haven't known Sam all that long but I think she would risk the possibility. She can use the premise, that to shut down without the normal precautions to abort, would jeopardize both target and investigator."

"I will ask her."

No—don't ask her—tell her. I'm in charge, unless I ask you to make the decision," said O'Malley.

"Aye, aye, my captain."

∞∞

21

Aborting the Sweep

The director of the FBI glared at his deputy. "Have you told them to shut that show down?"

"Yes, Sir. I've made it clear your directive is to be obeyed, or there will be consequences. But I want to know why you are so adamant about it. What harm can it do, to complete the sweep?"

For God's sake, Don—its a pandora's box. Didn't you think it through? The repercussions for liability are legion."

"I had a judge agree to the first sweep with an injunction. We caught Coulson because of it," Hadley complained.

"May I remind you that the FBI did not catch Coulson. He was caught by a bunch of useless, homeless people, and besides, catching Coulson by these means was not a priority.

We would have caught him eventually, but now—with this box of magic tricks we're opening ourselves up to God knows what."

"Coulson gave consent for his memory to be investigated. He can't claim any right of way. All O'Malley is after is information."

"Coulson probably acted on his own, anyway. There's no indication of a conspiracy to assassinate him, is there?"

"Neither the NSA, or the CIA have come up with anything, but I doubt Coulson acted alone."

"Well, we'll get to the bottom of it—and without this new-fangled technology. I spoke to the acting president this afternoon and he also feels we should not pursue this direction. The technology's future needs to be discussed by an independent panel of law experts before it can be used to solve crime."

"I must go to the Institute and make sure the order is complied with," said Hadley.

"Speak to the dean and warn him of the consequences."

"I will, don't worry."

*

Samantha turned to Lucas with a surprised look. "O'Malley has refused to obey the request. I must say, I'm not surprised."

Lucas smiled thinly. "Let's hope the assistant director doesn't arrive to enforce the order."

"It's out of our hands, ducky. I can't throw the switch. It'll harm both of them."

"Just tell Hadley, if he does join us, we have started the abort procedure, but it takes time."

The lab door opened and the dean walked in accompanied by Don Hadley.

"Speak of the devil," said Samantha.

Hadley pushed past the dean and stood at the console. "You must shut this thing down right now."

"Go take long walk off a short peer," said Samantha.

"You can't speak to me like that, Miss Pink. I am the assistant director of the FBI."

"I just did, asshole. I can't shut the operation down. It could harm both these men. I don't care about Coulson, but O'Malley's a good man."

"Special Agent O'Malley understood the risks. The FBI director is acting on the order of the acting president of the United States. He says, shut it down."

"Over my dead body,"said Samantha.

"I can arrange that,"said Hadley.

The dean stepped in to mitigate the argument. "We're not getting anywhere with this, Mr. Hadley. We've explained the dangers and you refuse to listen to reason. I am asking you to leave the premises."

Hadley gave him a stoney glare. "I'll pull that power plug out of the wall if I have to. Now, for the last time, Miss Pink—shut it down, before I get mad."

Samantha gave him a long, hard look and sat down at the console. She typed in some instructions.

"Now we must wait. I take no responsibility for what happens next." she said.

*

O'Malley sensed, in his semi-state, something to be wrong. His right brain thoughts were being clouded by a picture, conjured up by the left brain consciousness. It gave him an overwhelming feeling of danger. An emergency situation in the laboratory needed to be addressed. Somehow, he needed to take care of it.

"Urgent message from Sam, Dillon."

"What does she say?"

She seems really upset. Apparently your boss Hadley is there, commanding her to pull the plug on the operation, despite the risks of damaging your mental state."

"What does she want us to do?"

"She says you have to will yourself back into your left brain consciousness and momentarily withdraw from the avatar."

"I didn't know that was possible."

"It is possible, but only from a theoretical point of view. Scientifically, your two hemispheres will still be separated by distance but the quantum enigma allows for your right brain to move all its mental acuity back to the left for a brief period. We had never considered this to be a viable option but it may actually work."

"What will I do if I am able to achieve this?"

"Stop Hadley from doing what he has in his mind to do—to pull the power plug out of the wall socket. Sam told him she's busy shutting the avatar down but instead has sent a message to warn us. You must act quickly."

The nature of O'Malley's career often produced situations in which he found himself backed against a wall. All his training on the psychology behind dealing with uncertainty and decision-making, came to the fore, in a concerted effort to answer the query of how to do the impossible. He knew what he had to do but he didn't know how to achieve it.

Echo came to the rescue. *"Think about the details of Sam's message, Dillon. Think in terms of fusing those details into the larger picture and what the outcome of Hadley's actions will mean for us."*

O'Malley thought detail. "I'm thinking of Sam at the computer console, speaking to Hadley—I'm thinking of the experiment and the shutdown of the avatar—I am trying to draw it into a consequence."

"Keep each of your detailed thoughts in view and imagine a plus sign inbetween, pulling them toward each other. Imagine the final impression of consequence and cause— make it pulsate in your mind's eye, like a disco sign."

"What am I trying to achieve?"

"You're trying to make your right-brain consciousness think like your left brain does. We will see if the quantum effect of entanglement will not draw part of the right brain

back to the brain's combined hemispherical operation."

*

Dots of perspiration, like a sprinkler system, popped out on Hadley's brow. This glorified young pussycat was pushing his buttons and he could feel the bile rising in his throat. The angina pills should help regulate heartbeat caused by his rising emotions. He felt for the tablets but realized the small container resided in one of his jacket pockets. The jacket lay on the backseat of his car.

He glared at Samantha. "The responsibility for the outcome lies with the Acting President and the director of the FBI."

His eyes showed strain and the overweight body shuddered with anger. Hadley had not been well since the minor heart attack, seven months prior. He coughed and spluttered but would not back down. To make his intention known he stepped over to the wall plug socket where the three phase power cable plugged into the wall.

"I don't trust you. If this doesn't end in the next minute I'll pull this cord out."

Lucas moved threateningly toward Hadley. "I wouldn't do that if I were you. The avatar will breakup and a part of O'Malley's consciousness might be lost. Coulson will also suffer radiation effects from the disbanded particles—the outcome will not be good for either of them."

"I understand your concerns, Professor, but we can't ignore the Acting President's order. The truth of the matter is you are probably more concerned about the experiment than the welfare of either of these men—you also don't seem certain about the outcome of this shutdown. Maybe it would be a good time to find out."

A sudden hush fell over the lab as the two parties faced off against each other. A voice broke the impasse. "Step away from that cable, Don."

Hadley reacted as though he had been slapped in the face. They turned and stared at the speaker—O'Malley, still seated in his chair with his eyes glazed and face the color of ash, stared back at Hadley. The Glock, removed from its holster, pointed at the deputy director's chest. The voice, strained and barely audible croaked out the message with firm resolution.

"I mean it, Don. I will shoot you if you try to pull that cord out of its socket."

The cord, a thick cable with a large three-pronged plug and secured by a slide-over locking device, would require a certain amount of effort to be removed. Hadley looked like a wounded dog caught in an animal trap. For a moment the others thought he might try to remove the cable but a reaction set in to his cardiac system and he stared to convulse. The strain, with its accompanying emotion, became too much for him. He let go of the cable and dropped onto his knees. His face turned a pale color as the heart attack took hold and started to shut his cardiac system down.

Lucas turned to the dean. "Quick, call 911. This man is having a heart attack."

Hadley toppled onto his stomach. His eyes bulged and he fought to draw air into his lungs. He clutched at his throat as Samantha jumped in to help Lucas roll the assistant director onto his back. Lucas pulled off his tie and loosened the shirt collar. The dean called 911 and opened the lab door to enquire if anyone had first aid experience. One of the guards came forward and began CPR.

Hadley passed out and the guard continued his efforts while Samantha and Lucas stood back. They both recalled the final minutes that lead up to the assistant director's unfortunate event and simultaneously shout the name —"O'Malley."

Samantha reached the special agent first and stare down at him. O'Malley's arm dangled downward and the Glock lay beside the chair.

'He's returned to the avatar," said Samantha.

"Your little ruse worked—well done, Sam." Lucas lifted one of O'Malley's eyelids to see the pupil rolled back into the socket.

"I took a chance that Echo would realize what to do—she's so smart."

"You're so clever, pussycat," said Lucas.

The dean intervened. "911 are on their way. I hope they make it in time, however, I can see problems for us if Hadley pulls through."

Lucas picked up O'Malley's Glock and replaced it in its holster. "According to the three of us, this didn't happen the way it did," he whispered.

The guard who administered the CPR stood up and wiped his brow. "I've got a pulse. I think he'll be okay."

In the distance they could hear the sirens as the ambulance made its way toward the Institute.

Lucas referred to the irony of their situation. "It seems every time we do this experiment there's some sort of collateral damage."

"We've been saved by a heart attack. The dick had it coming to him," said Samantha.

The dean raised his eyes. "Now, now, Sam— he was only following orders."

The guard stepped into the corridor to inform the others about the deputy director's fate. Lucas lowered his voice and said, "No one knows exactly what transpired here except us. We can finish off the sweep, providing O'Malley's okay. The director of the FBI will be none the wiser and we'll tell him that the experiment was shut down under Hadley's orders."

"But what will happen when Hadley revives and tells his story?" Samantha asked.

"O'Malley will have to deal with it. Either way, the information will be recorded and it's not something we need to tell the director of the FBI about," said Lucas.

"Agreed," said the dean.

Samantha ran her hand through O'Malley's bushy hair. "I'm just glad our friend came to no harm. We've also accomplished some mind-bending discoveries which will help with the future application of the sweep."

Lucas smiled. "Despite the collateral damage we still win. Let's get on with the monitoring process." ∞∞

22

Back to Reality

O'Malley's view from the avatar returned with a transition from darkness to dim luminescence. He had sensed the intervention of an extraordinary event which pulled at his mind, to transport his consciousness into another place. His recall of the 'other place' floated in a murky sea of intuition and revealed only a fleeting glimpses of his boss, Don Hadley, standing with an electrical cable in hand.

"Echo—Are you still with me?"

"Welcome back, sweetie. I'v missed you."

"Do you know what just happened?"

"You were successful in transporting your consciousness back to the lab. According to Sam you prevented your boss, Don Hadley, from pulling the plug on the sweep."

O'Malley tried to recall more detail but it wouldn't come. "It's vague but I remember seeing Hadley standing at a wall with a cable in his hand."

"*You pulled your revolver out and threatened to shoot him if he didn't let go of the cable.*"

"Did he?"

"*Sam says the boss had a heart attack as he was about to pull the cable. He will be okay, it appears. 911 has arrived to take him to the hospital.*"

"I don't know how I'll explain my way out of this. I take it Sam is not shutting the sweep down, then?"

"*No, they feel you should carry on and finish what has been started.*"

"Where exactly are we?"

"*We have entered a newer area of memory. Tell me what you are visualizing right now.*"

O'Malley peered within his virtual realm. "I see what looks like a courtroom and there are a group of military officers, sitting at a bench,

facing me. Next to me are two other officers, in military uniform. The one appears to be a lawyer of sorts."

"Can you hear what the officer is saying, Dillon?"

"He is asking for permission for the other officer to speak. The officer is giving his rank and name—Colonel Leif Hansen, U.S. Marine Corps."

Without warning the scene started to dim and blur. O'Malley knew the cause of it.

"Echo? We have blurring again. I guess Coulson has realized the avatar has moved on and we are attempting to access this particular memory."

"Give me a moment, my king. I will let Sam know—perhaps she can do something about it."

O'Malley watched as the dim and blurred images deteriorate further. A moment later the scene became a vague blur. He waited.

After interminable seconds, the scene suddenly brightened and morphed back to a clear picture again.

"We have the scene again. Sam must have done something drastic—I don't fancy being in Coulson's shoes."

"She must have provided a means of distraction he couldn't ignore. Just as well—there is nothing we can do from our side."

For ten minutes O'Malley watched courtroom proceedings and listened to the conversation.

"They have just acquitted Coulson of blame for the friendly-fire incident. Twenty-three Canadians died as a result of his judgement call, but his commanding officer is saying he did not receive a certain communication regarding the Canadian presence, due to a radio malfunction."

"What do you make of it, o' great one?"

"It's worth remembering. If we're looking for reasons of how Coulson might be black-mailed—there may be something in this incident. I'm sure a radio signal came through to warn him of the Canadian presence."

The scene faded out as the avatar moved through the field of memory and entered a new one. The luminescence, which surrounded them turned a deeper violet color. O'Malley realized their progress embraced the more well-formed memories of the long term type and not incidental issues, which could be recalled for a short term only. The avatar advanced toward the latest memories which accounted for the changes in color.

"Tell me which memories you would like to pay closer attention to as we pass through and I will slow the avatar down, my captain."

O'Malley saw some details privy to the secret service commissions, Coulson had been on. He also saw the deaths of Veronica and Gracie Beauchamp, which he did not wish to view and allowed the avatar to keep a steady pace through the areas, until they reached a specific scene.

"Slow us down—I want to see this."

The avatar slowed to a snail's pace and O'-Malley stared at a piece of paper in Coulson's hand. The blackmailer, with text cut from old magazines or newspapers, cried out to him from the print. He read it out allowed for the record.

"...*You will make your way to the shower room on the top floor, overlooking the main hall. In the shower room you will find and unused 180mm pipe, sticking out of the wall. It extends from the old decommissioned boiler room, next door to the showers. The pipe has a blind flange closing it off. Inside the third locker you will find an adjustable spanner on the top shelve. Undo the bolts of the blind and remove it. Inside the pipe you will find the weapon, wrapped in plastic...* "

A distant bell rang in the back of his mind but he could not place the twinge of suspicion regarding the use of words. An out-of-place concept tangled with his knowledge of linguistics but he could not put his finger on it. Perhaps it came down to a left-right brain thing and he couldn't sum up the obvious.

"Let's move on, Echo. I think I've seen everything I need here."

"Aye, aye, my captain."

The avatar picked up speed and soon O'-Malley recognized flashes of the most recent memories, up to the apprehension of Coulson, by the team of FBI policemen.

"'I think we're done, Echo. You can tell Sam to pull us out now. I'm not sure how productive the whole mission was but the record may still produce something."

"At your command, my sweetie."

The avatar moved at a pace, which O'Malley noticed did not match the speed, before the glial cell attack.

"Are we going to be in any danger because of our reduced speed?"

"We're not far from the exit point but we'll have to watch any crossing of synapse gaps, between the chosen axons and their corresponding dendrites."

The avatar crossed over three more synapse gaps. Protective glials moved toward them but the cells, not close enough for direct confrontation could not stage any attacks, before the avatar moved into the relevant dendrites.

"You can relax, my sweetie. We're home and dry."

"As my wife says—home again, home again, jiggerty-jig," said O'Malley. His relief knew no bounds. Once outside the brain, the avatar lurched forward and with a rush, resumed the normal speed of the particle accelerator's continuum.

*

"Wakey, wakey, Dillon." Samantha's voice sounded muffled.

O'Malley could here her but she sounded far off, at first. He opened his eyes to see the smiling faces of the dean, Samantha and Lucas, all waiting to see him released from the bonds of the avatar."God, I've got a headache— I feel as though I've been through a cement-mixer," said O'Malley.

"It's quite normal. You'll take a while to adjust," said Lucas.

Samantha released the clamp on the head harness and swung the contraption to one side. O'Malley looked across at Coulson who appeared to be asleep.

"What happened to him?"

The dean laughed. "Sam got a bit carried away when Echo sent a message regarding his resistance to your efforts. She jumped up from the console, grabbed a spare support bar from the accelerator and whacked him on the back of the head."

"She could have killed him," said Lucas.

"I knew she had done something drastic. The dimming and blurring of the images disappeared without warning and I could see again."

The dean became serious. "I'm concerned for your sake, though. Hadley started to create quite a scene and I was scared Sam might throw something at him. He wanted the mission terminated immediately. We were between a rock and a hard place."

O'Malley scowled. "I have scant memory of the ordeal." he felt for the Glock and gave a sigh of relief, when he found it still holstered.

Sam bit on her bottom lip. "You did threaten him with it. In fact you saved the situation because he was about to yank the cable out of its socket."

"Despite the fact he might have done both Coulson and I damage?" O'Malley asked.

"We warned him of the problems. He didn't care—said he and the director would take the responsibility."

"How bad is Hadley's condition?" O'Malley asked.

"The paramedics stabilized him and were pretty sure he would live," said Lucas.

"It creates a problem for me. Don't get me wrong—I'm glad he didn't croak but it would have been better for my future if he had."

Samantha gave an evil smile. "I'm one hundred percent with you, sweetie."

"You sound just like Echo when you say that," said O'Malley.

"She's got more silicon in her brain than you can imagine." Lucas quipped.

Samantha gave him a playful punch on the shoulder. "Your hard drive is corrupted, again, worm-breath."

The dean looked peeved. "Children, children—give us a break. We need to help the special agent resolve this problem."

O'Malley thought about the repercussions. "I'm sure Hadley will remember the incident. I could mount a defense but I'm not sure the director will take my side. There are severe penalties for agents who threaten their own, with a weapon."

Lucas folded his arms. "What's the worst scenario? You have our testimony that we warned him. We will tell him the mission was shut down straight after the incident, but with care."

"I think the worst case scenario is my suspension from duty until the issue is resolved. It seems strange the director wanted it shut down so quickly."

"Do you think the sweep was worthwhile?" The dean asked.

"I didn't see anything that jumped out but there are a few things which bothered me and I will need to see the records once you have them."

"I'll work on those right away, in case the FBI want to commandeer the setup," said Samantha.

"We need to release Coulson back into custody. He'll be moved from here to the penitentiary, to await his trial. I'll run the gauntlet with Hadley, pretty soon. I'll visit him in hospital and see how the land lies," said O'Malley.

He got to his feet with the help of Samantha and Lucas. "I need to give the guards instructions for Coulson's removal. Is he compos mentis?"

The dean walked over to observe Coulson and verified him to be awake.

∞∞

23

In the Aftermath

O'Malley thanked the dean for the ride home. Samantha had followed in O'Malley's Chevy, which she parked at the back of the apartment block. He still felt queazy and unbalanced from the effects of the sweep but would not accept any further help and he wobbled up the stairs, unassisted, to the second floor. Lucas assured him the effects would be gone by the next morning. What to tell Janet would be the real dilemma. She knew nothing of the sweep or the Institute, save that he met there with some of the staff, to discuss the Gracie Beauchamp case. She never pried into his business.

Janet greeted him from the kitchen as he entered the apartment and he went to peck her on the cheek. "Hi, honey. Excuse me while I take a shower."

She looked a little put out. "Dinner will be ready in half-an-hour."

"Okay," he shouted. The cool water felt good on his face.

"Breaking news said that Don Hadley had a heart attack today. Were you with him at the time?"

O'Malley thought it might make the late-night news but the journalistic grapevine travelled fast.

"Yes, hon. We were at the Institute when it happened. The paramedics arrived in good time and took him to the hospital. They say he should be okay."

O'Malley returned to the kitchen. He sat at the table and without warning the room began to spin. He placed his head in his hands and waited for it to pass.

"What's wrong sweetheart? Janet asked. She shot him a look of alarm.

"Oh, it's nothing—I'm probably tired."

"You are looking a little pale around the gills. Not getting enough sleep?"

"Could be."

"Thinking about Fallon again?"

"I guess so." The line of questions began to irritate him.

"Want to talk about it?"

"No."

"You're shutting me out again, Dillon."

I'm not shutting you out—I just don't want to talk about it."

"You need to talk about it, to somebody."

"Yeah, I know, but not now. Please let me relax. It's been a harrowing day."

"This is always going to be a problem between us. If our counseling is not working out then you need to find someone else to help you. God knows, I can't do this anymore."

"Come on, Jan. Don't make a big thing of this now. Give me a few hours and I'll be alright."

She stepped over to the oven and pulled down the door to check on the roast. He noticed her shapely figure and how tight the jeans pulled over her well-formed buttocks. It had been a while since they had made love and he came to a firm realization—he did not want to lose her.

O'Malley stood up and moved around the table to place his arms around her but the room started to spin again. She turned to catch him in her arms as he keeled over sideways.

"What's happening, honey? You look quite ashen. Is the wound in your arm worrying you?"

"Sorry, love. I need to lie down for a while. I feel a bit light-headed."

"Do I need to get you to the doctor?"

"No. It's nothing and it will pass. Please don't fuss."

She assisted him to the bedroom and helped him down onto the bed. "You need to sleep. I'll keep dinner for you in case you're hungry when you wake up."

"Thank's, hon." He closed his eyes and passed out.

*

The director of the FBI sat around the table in a Pentagon boardroom, with two other people .

"What's the current state of affairs?" General Leif Hansen asked.

The director rubbed his chin. "Hadley ordered them to shut the probe down minutes before his heart attack."

The person they referred to as 'Angel', spoke. "Do you think they shut it down?"

"I really have no way of knowing. I've asked for an audit of the Institute's master control computer, the one which apparently runs the memory-sweep program. One of our IT specialists will be doing that today," said the director.

"What will that prove?" Angel asked.

"It will tell us how long they ran the program for and if any extra-ordinary record was kept, of what O"Malley saw," said Hansen.

Did Hadley see anything before the process was shut down?" Angel asked.

"Because one of the physicists, a woman—refused to comply with my order, Hadley was about to pull the power plug to the accelerator—but O'Malley woke up and threatened him with a weapon. The heart attack happened immediately after," said the director.

"It indicates the possibility of the continuation of the sweep. If Hadley passed out he wouldn't know what happened afterwards," said Angel.

One of the FBI policemen conducted CPR on Hadley and said the equipment still appeared to be in operation. But you are correct. We don't really know."

"This is a revolutionary concept which, according to the dean of the Institute, was never meant for solving crimes," said Hansen.

Angel glared at Hansen. "It's not good news for us despite the contribution to science—I understand it will win the inventors a nobel prize but we can't afford any discovery the agent might have made, to leak out."

The director held Angel's gaze. "I still say Coulson didn't know anything which could incriminate us."

"I would hate to take the chance of Coulson's lack of information and then find out he has some distant memory of the friendly-fire incident, which could lead authorities to the plot and sink us," retorted Hansen.

"Take it easy, Leif. I'm in control of the situation. We'll see if O'Malley knows anything and take it from there," said the director.

'What about Hadley?" Hansen asked.

"The assistant director knows nothing. I'll handle it."

Angel smiled thinly. "It's your O'Malley I'm worried about. I think we should make sure—can't you eliminate him?"

"What about the dean and the two physicists? You think we should just eliminate them too?" The director asked.

"It would raise too many eyebrows." said Hansen.

"Let me handle it. I'll arrange for something to be done if we suspect any trouble from these people, O'Malley included," said the director. He stood to indicate the end of their meeting. "In the mean time I suggest you both calm down and stop jumping to conclusions."

*

O'Malley made his way to the hospital. The two hours sleep helped his condition enough for him to maintain balance again. Janet, not impressed with his attitude, took their son, Steven, to see a movie and left a note about the left over dinner. He couldn't stand the thought of eating, scraped the dinner into the garbage and left to pay his boss, Don Hadley, a visit.

He walked into the hospital foyer and noticed the time—7:45 p.m. The corridors pulsated with busy people. Nurse-aids scurried to check on patients and doctors with anxious expressions bounded up stairs, to the floors above. O'Malley enquired as to Hadley's ward and the receptionist directed him to the sixth floor. He steeled himself to face his boss.

Hadley's closed eyes suggested he might be asleep when O'Malley walked in and stood by the bed. The special agent remained standing until Hadley, after a few moments, cranked open an eyelid and acknowledged his presence.

"Sit, O'Malley. We have something to discuss."

"Yes, we do, Don. I want to say I would never have shot you. I only wanted to allow Samantha to close the operation down properly."

"You threatened a senior officer with your weapon, Dillon. That's a fireable offense."

"You threatened to pull the plug and ruin my brain," said O'Malley.

"You seem perfectly sane to me."

"Only because Sam was able to shut the process down correctly. I don't understand why shutting down the sweep became suddenly so important."

"The order came from the acting President of the United States. The director made it clear we should never have entered into the experiment in the first place."

"The director was off at the time. You're the one who takes the responsibility for any ramifications," said O'Malley. He could feel his Irish ire rising.

"I didn't see any harm in it at the time—we needed to apprehend Coulson and find out who was behind the assassination," said Hadley.

"We shouldn't be arguing about this, Don. You're not in any shape to get your hackles up. The order to abort was obeyed and nothing much came of Coulson's sweep."

"I'm glad to hear that." Relief reflected in the assistant director's voice. "However, the director wanted to know what happened and I told him what you did."

O'Malley shrugged. "No one got killed so there's no big deal."

"I just gave him the facts, Dillon. He wants to have a meeting with you."

"Fine by me," said O'Malley.

"He's having the master computer which runs the program, checked by one of the IT staff. I hope you shut it down as you said, because he is bound to find out."

"There was nothing that I saw which gave me any leads on the assassination plot and Coulson agreed to the procedure. I didn't violate his rights."

The director is concerned about the longterm fallout from this. He says a panel of experts should be vetting the procedure."

O'Malley relaxed. "Are you feeling okay, Don?"

"Yeah, I'm good. It will take me a while to get over the fact you threatened to shoot me, however, it's the director I'm worried about—watch your back, Dillon."

"Thank's for the advice. Are we good?"

The deputy director stared up into O'Malley's face and hesitated. "Yeah we're good. But if you ever pull a stunt like that again, I'll kick your ass from here to China."

O'Malley grinned. "Point taken. I must go now—Janet should be home from the movies soon."

"Look after yourself, Dillon." he turned over and closed his eyes.

O'Malley took the elevator down to the ground floor and made his way out to the carpark. A few adverse effects still remained in his system and on occasion he felt a floating sensation, but it lasted for only a brief second or two.

Janet waited in the living room for him. "Where's Steve?" He asked.

"He's in his room. You and I need to talk, Dillon."

O'Malley groaned within himself and sat down.

"Hows the assistant director ," she asked.

"Recovering well and looking good. He'll be retiring soon—I think he deserves the rest."

Janet fidgeted with her blouse and then folded her hands. "I feel we've reached the end of the line, Dillon. We don't talk any more and I haven't a clue on how to rectify this huge chasm between us. You don't make love to me anymore and while I understand you have a job to do it's at the expense of everything else.

"Jan..."

"No. please don't say anything—let me finish. I know how keenly you feel our daughter's death. I know you blame yourself to an extent. You've shut Steve and I out. We are trying to get on with the rest of our lives but you're trapped inside a cocoon of misery. I love you, Dillon. But our lives are a mess and no amount of counsel seems to help. You fling yourself, daily, into your job and maybe you get some sort of temporary relief.

"Jan..."

"Shut up, Dillon. I'm still talking. You're suffering a type of PTSD and you need help. I can't stay around you while you are like this. I'm taking Steve and we're going to my mother's for a while. Please use the time to get yourself right."

O'Malley could sense her frustration. He wanted to get up and hold her but he knew it would be the wrong thing to do. He bowed his head and allowed the rising anger to ebb. It would not be helpful for him to go off the deep end at her.

"How long will you be gone?"

"For as long as it takes," she said. Janet stood and walked with purpose toward the door. "Please don't contact me until you've dealt with your fears."

When will I ever see my son?" O'Malley asked.

"Every Friday , after school comes out. He can come home for the weekends if your busy work schedule allows it. I don't want to come between you and Steven, Dillon. A boy needs his father."   ∞∞

24

A Meeting with the Director.

O'Malley sat in the director's office and waited. Fifteen minutes later the man strode in and without offering a greeting sat behind his desk. O'Malley narrowed his eyelids and braced himself for a barrage of questions. After what seemed an eternity the director looked up and eyed the special agent.

"Tell me about your little excursion at the Institute. What did you learn about Coulson's motives?"

O'Malley blinked and looked at his hands which were folded on his lap. "Not very much that will help us solve the real crime."

The director raised an eyebrow. "The real crime?"

"The conspiracy to assassinate the President."

"Are you confident there was a conspiracy?"

"Coulson did not act alone. He received letters of instructions from a blackmailer," said O'Malley.

"And you actually saw these letters—what did they look like?"

"They were cutouts from magazines. Pasted together to form messages."

"What else did you see?"

O'Malley did not want to give anything more away. "Nothing."

The director stared at him for a few moments, the silence palpable.

"Just so you know, we've taken the computer's record. My IT department tell me if a file has been deleted. I imagine Miss Pink, or professor Wheeler, would have something to do with that."

O'Malley made no comment.

"The record reveals the sweep went on for quite a while after Hadley was removed by the

paramedics but there is no content. Are you trying to hide something, O'Malley?"

"No, Sir. Why would I try to hide anything? It's true, the sweep continued on for a short while, but the dean made the decision to continue. He did so, because Coulson and I could have been irreparably harmed, due to a sudden shut down of the system."

"So you say," said the director. His voice contained a measure of sarcasm. "Which brings me to the issue of you and Hadley. You deliberately pulled a weapon on a senior office and threatened to shoot him. No matter the circumstance, we can't condone this type of behavior. I am suspending you, pending a full investigation on the matter. Please hand over your badge and gun."

O'Malley had suspected as much. "How long is this likely to take, Sir?"

"It's difficult to say, but you will receive full pay until the matter is sorted out, so take a vacation. You are off the case until further notice.

Unfortunately, you need to find alternative means of transportation—we need the Chevy."

O'Malley stared at the director for several moments before he handed over the Glock and his badge. This would be a blow to any further advancement in his career. He could not see the reason, however, behind the director's decision to shut down the current investigation. There appeared to be a total disregard for the facts already gathered by the sweep. O'Malley could also understand the need for enforcement of FBI protocol in the matter of his pulling a gun on a senior officer, but the director ignored the conditions under which it took place. Was the director making an attempt to cover something up?

He stood and turned toward the door. "I don't understand why you are doing this, Sir."

"Trust me, O'Malley. This is for the best."

The special agent shook his head in disbelief and left the director's office. He told the secretary of the department he would be on leave for a while and left the building. O'Leary's pub, two blocks from J.Edgar Hoover would provide him a place and an opportunity, to think things through. There seemed no point in going home to an empty apartment.

Four pints later he saw the world through different eyes. The more he thought about the current position, the more he sensed fowl-play. Fueled by a few more beers his intuition flared into conspiracy theories and plots, driving him relentlessly into an angry frame of mind. At eleven pm the bartender, an old friend of O'-Malley's, came over to provide a word of comfort.

"Hope you're not driving, Dillon."

"Naw—I'll get a cab," he said.

"Can I call you one?"

"Yeah, I guess I've drunk enough for one evening."

The bartender picked up the phone and dialed for the service. O'Malley got unsteadily to his feet. Despite the inebriated state his observation skills still came to the fore as he looked around the crowded room. A man in the far corner, sipping on his drink, looked away suddenly when O'Malley's eyes fell upon him. The split-second in which he eyed the man, before the stranger averted his gaze, confirmed the man had been watching him. O'Malley's gaze lingered a little longer than it should have and alerted the stranger he had become aware.

The man continued to sip on his drink and focused his attention on another area of the bar. The bartender confirmed the cab service. "Your ride will be waiting outside by the time you've had a pee, Dillon."

O'Malley thanked him and walked with unsteady legs to the bathroom. Several people needed to empty their bladders at the same time and he needed to wait in a short lineup, before he could relieve himself. The cab waited at the curb and as he sat down in the back seat to give the address, he realized the stranger had not been sitting in the corner when he passed through the bar, on his way to the exit. The cabbie acknowledged the address and pulled out into the traffic. O'Malley relaxed.

He let his head loll back on the seat, closed his eyes and tried not to think about anything.

The taxi came to a sudden stop, jerking him out of the melodramatic thoughts which swirled around in his mind.

"You're home, boss. That'll be thirty-one dollars."

O'Malley reached into a pocket and pulled out his wallet. After yanking out several notes he crammed them into the driver's out-stretched hand. The driver looked at the notes and smiled—O'Malley had mistaken twenties for tens.

"Keep the change," said O'Malley. His words slurred a little, but at least he could walk straight. The taxi-driver drove away, con-tented.

O'Malley squinted at the double-glass doors of the apartment's foyer and felt around in his wallet for the key. After two attempts he man-aged to find the keyhole. The apartment block did not have an elevator so he made his way to the stairwell, but stopped at the letterbox, to

check for post. With several bills clutched in his one hand he pulled himself upward, two steps at a time with the other hand, until he reached the first-floor landing. He paused for a brief rest and then walked to his apartment's door.

The door lock provided no resistance to the key and it swung open at the turn of the handle.

"That's weird," mused O'Malley.

Certain he had locked the door on his departure that morning, a warning bell rang in his mind and he called loudly, "Janet, are you here?"

No answer. He no longer had the comfort of the Glock. He slipped into the kitchen, from the hallway, opened a drawer and pulled out a carving knife; the one which he used to carve up the turkey on Thanksgiving, every year. The apartment's lights remained off and by the indirect glow of light from the street, he could see vague shapes of the furniture in the living room. The hallway which led to the three bed

rooms revealed the door-jambs of each room's entrance, but nothing more. O'Malley sensed the presence of another person and in an instant he sobered up, with the realization his life might be in danger.

"I know someone is in here. You'd better identify yourself." His voice sounded strange to him. The only sounds filtered up through the living room windows, from the street below. He listened intently but couldn't hear anything out of the ordinary. Taking a deep breath he stepped out of the kitchen and into the living room, proper, with the knife held out in front of him. A noise, to the right caught the immediate focus of his attention. O'Malley felt two strong arms grab him on the opposite side from where the noise had first emanated. This ploy, used in FBI training, situations raised suspicion as to who the attacker might be—another operative, perhaps? In a darkened area, an object would be thrown across the room, to make a noise and thereby draw the quarry's attention.

O'Malley dropped onto his knees and rolled over. He managed to break the hold for a brief

second and slip one arm free, before his assailant re-situated the bearhug and continued to squeeze the breath out him.

He tried to swing his knife-hand but the arm, stilled pinned to his side, could not gain sufficient movement and his adversary's shear strength made it impossible to break the hold. The attacker made a quick move to dislodge the knife, which fell to the floor. O'Malley's training took over and he swiveled his free arm over his head and caught the back of his assailants cranium. He groped for the man's ear and twisted as hard as he could. He heard a grunt of pain and the man lessened his grip, which gave O'Malley an opportunity to turn the tables. The attacker, however, appeared to possess a good knowledge of hand-to-hand combat and countered O'Malley's attempt to gain a firm neck-hold.

A fist smashed into the side of his face and almost dislodged a molar. Warm blood flowed inside his mouth and he spat it out, into the man's face. As they writhed around on the carpet, O'Malley felt the man maneuver, to gain a position behind him in order to grab his head

and apply the death-twist, but the special agent had other ideas. In a slip and roll movement O'Malley managed to push his opponent away from him and jump to his feet. He let loose a round-house kick which nearly dislodged the man's head and followed up with two straight punches.

The attacker, caught off guard, realized the tide of the battle was turning in O'Malley's favor and he let go a kick at the special agent's knee. O'Malley winced in pain but continued his forward momentum to grab at the man's sweater. His assailant warded off the motion and ran into the hallway, toward the front door of the apartment. The door slammed in O'Malley's face as he tried to follow. He lost precious seconds, in an attempt to grab the door handle, while his assailant fled to the landing and leapt down the stairs, three at a time. When O'Malley reached the landing the man had burst through the double-doors in the foyer and out onto the street.

O'Malley stood on the landing and decided he would not attempt to pursue the man any further. His breath came in gasps as he gulped for

air and he realized his fitness level could be better. More time needed to be spent in the FBI gym. The attacker had not been sent to rob him, but to kill him. He thought about the tactic used to distract his attention in one of the earlier maneuvers of the battle. It proved one thing—the attacker's combat training had to be either Military, CIA or FBI. His suspicions, with regard to the director's complicity in this failed attempt to take his life, took a firm hold on his mind. The shutdown of the memory sweep and his consequent suspension, left him with one thought—a coverup.

He returned to the apartment and sat at the kitchen table while he waited for the coffeemaker to produce a strong brew of caffein. Someone had tried to kill him. Why? The answer came as an epiphany—certain people did not want Coulson's thoughts on display. He, O'Malley, could provide some evidence which might lead to the killer, or killers, of President Lewis and that is why they wanted to get rid of him. He chided himself for releasing information to Hadley and the director, in particular the visual of the blackmail letters. The letters contained some sort of clue as to the identity of the conspirators.

Another thought crossed his mind. The killers would be after all those involved in the sweep of Coulson's memory.

∞∞

25

Hiding the Information

Samantha Pink sat at her desk and enjoyed the warm rays of the morning sun, as they filtered through the lab's window. In her hand she held a memory stick which contained the file of the Coulson memory sweep. The FBI's visit on the previous afternoon had done little to placate her concerns, regarding the security and safety of the sweep program. A belligerent FBI agent, who called himself Allan Morris, had stopped by to pick up her computer, which she released under extreme duress. The dean intervened when he heard the commotion, caused by the tussle for her laptop, accompanied by her extreme string of expletives and offensive remarks.

The agent, after threats about non-cooperation and incarceration, got his way in the end. Despite the dean's threat of suing the Bureau for violation of the Institute's intellectual property, and Samantha threatening to cut out his private parts, the agent managed to make his case. They would not find anything of importance and it didn't matter if they looked at the files of Gracie Beauchamp's sweep, which render information already documented. The success of the program spoke for its self , however, the Institute would not invite any further use for the purpose of solving crime. The potential for abuse could be too great and a federal court judge would need to make a ruling.

On the day in question, Samantha and Lucas down-loaded the finished file of Coulson's sweep, onto a memory stick and then she erased the record on the computer's hard drive. The FBI would know she erased the file but they would never know its contents. O'-Malley warned her the director would want all the details and she should make a plan to secure the information.

"That stupid FBI guy, Morris, can go and suck oranges. There's no way he's going to get his hands on this information," said Samantha.

Lucas took the memory stick from her and turned it over in his hands. "I thought you were going to slam the laptop over his head, but seriously, what are we going to do with this."

"I'll take it home and hide it somewhere," she said.

"Not a good idea, Sam. If they really suspect we have this they'll turn your home upside down to find it. I know a good place." He picked up a small screwdriver and walked to the accelerator's power socket. Four small screws secured the power receptacle's cover plate and he proceeded to remove them.

"Isn't this a little bit of over-kill?" Samantha asked.

Lucas eyed her while he completed his task. "O'Malley was quite sure they wouldn't let things lie. There appears to be a reason why the director doesn't want any information, regarding the memory sweep, to remain as physical evidence."

"O'Malley spoke to you about that?"

"Immediately after the incident with Hadley, just before he left—he said the shutting down of the sweep seemed suspicious. According to his reckoning, someone high up wanted to eradicate any possibility of Coulson's memories, being on display."

"Do you think they'll come back, to make sure there's no backup?"

Lucas removed the power, cover plate from the wall and stuck the memory stick into the conduit, which held all the cables. He pressed the stick deep amongst the different colored cables, to ensure it remained hidden should someone pull the plate off, while conducting a quick search.

"I'm pretty sure of it. It won't take long for their IT guys to find out the file has been deleted. The dean, you and I, are the only ones who work in this lab."

"Do you think we're running a risk by withholding the info?"

"Possibly. I think we can trust O'Malley, though. It may not be a bad idea for us to take a short vacation—stay away for a while and see what transpires."

Samantha moved close to Lucas and placed her hand on his shoulder while he completed tightening up the cover's screws. "We can always go to one of those Mexican resorts and shack up together—just the two of us." She fluttered her eyes at him.

He gave her a stern look, then laughed. "You going to bring that cat of yours as a chaperone?"

She placed her hands on her hips. "You got the wrong pussy on the brain, Lucas."

She gave him a clout over the back of the head and sauntered back to her desk.

The phone rang to absorb the sudden stoney silence in the lab. Lucas grabbed it before Samantha could lean over to pick it up. He listened for a while and saw his eyes open wide.

Her inquisitiveness got the better of her. "What is it, Luke? What's happened?"

Lucas replaced the phone on its base and stared at her. "That was O'Malley. He says we're to leave the building, right away, and meet him at O'Leary's pub. Someone tried to kill him last night."

"Oh my God!" exclaimed Samantha. "Does he think our lives might be in danger?"

"He didn't say directly, but he implied it. We should get going."

"What about the dean?" Samantha asked.

"We'll have to inform him we'll be taking some leave. I doubt whether he will be in any danger."

"What are you waiting for then, Wheeler? Lets get out of here."

She threw off the lab-coat and picked up her purse, while Lucas grabbed his jacket. Together, they ran down the hall and out of a side door, into the carpark. Their quick flight saved them a confrontation with Agent Morris of the FBI who, after parking his car at the front en trance walked down the corridor with two men in his wake, toward the lab.

A matter of minutes separated the FBI and the two neurophysicists from what would have been an uncomfortable meeting. The Bentley fired up on the first turn of the ignition and Lucas spun the tires as they launched themselves out onto the street in the direction of O'Leary's pub.

*

Agent Morris stood at the window of the director's office and looked out across the city. "Did you do a proper search?" The director asked.

"Yes Sir. We came up with nothing."

"And the dean?"

"The dean doesn't know anything. He couldn't tell me where Wheeler and Pink had gone. He said they often took off together."

"And you found no hard drives, memory sticks or anything that might have been used to download the information?"

"They may have it on them, Sir. We just need to find them."

"Put out an APB on them," said the director. I wan't these two weirdos caught and brought in for questioning. They're definitely hiding something."

"Yes, Sir. I'll get our men onto it right away."

The director nodded and indicated the meeting to be at an end. Morris fled down the hallway to his own office and proceeded to give instructions for the APB.

The director closed his door and took a cell phone out of his bottom drawer. He dialed a number and waited. A voice answered after two rings.

"Mr. Director. To what do I owe the honor?"

The director leaned back in his chair and smoothed his greying hair with one hand.

"The professor and his little pussycat have made a sudden disappearance. What happened with O'Malley?"

The voice on the other end drawled on and the director's eyes narrowed into slits.

"That's not good news. How could your man have bungle it?"

*

Lucas parked the Bentley in a side-street, around the corner from O'Leary's. They walked into the pub and O'Malley, who sat alone in a corner near the back wall, beckoned to them.

"Hello, Professor, Samantha. Please take a seat."

Lucas sat opposite O'Malley while Samantha moved into the booth seat with the special agent. She leaned over and gave him a peck on the cheek. "How's my cuddly FBI guy, today?"

O'Malley blushed. "I don't feel very cuddly after last night, I'm afraid. Would either of you like something to drink?"

Lucas stood. "I'll get it, don't worry, Dillon. Sam—your usual?"

She nodded and moved right up close to O'Malley and jammed him against the wall. The special agent felt some pangs of embarrassment but shrugged it off. "Poor baby, you look as though you haven't slept a wink," she said.

"In fact I have slept very little and I have some bad news for you and Lucas."

Lucas returned with their drinks and plonked himself down, across the table from them. "So what's this bad news, Dillon? You said someone tried to kill you last night."

O'Malley recounted the story of his suspension and then the attempt on his life. "I believe there is a conspiracy of some sort going on and it has to do with the assassination of President Lewis."

"Did you find anything of importance while perusing Coulson's memories?" Lucas asked.

I have given it a great deal of thought and there is something. It may not be significant— yet, one of the memories keeps coming back to my mind and I can't shake it."

"What memory is that, sweetie?" Samantha placed her hand over O'Malley's and in a strange way he felt comforted by it.

"It's to do with the blackmail letters. There were three in all, the physical evidence of which no longer exists. The text for the letters was taken from the same source—it maybe a magazine, or a newspaper."

Samantha could not stop her insatiable need to know all the details. "What about the text?"

"They looked as though they were from English magazines."

Lucas frowned. "By English, you mean British, English?

"Yes. I know this because of the spelling of some words. The text contained several words which are spelled differently from American English. For example, the use of metric for pipe sizes—one of the letters mentioned a 180mm pipe, which would be six inches in the US. Another part of the same letter talks about behavior but spelled the British way, with a 'u.' Reference is also made to an 'adjustable spanner', which would be an adjustable wrench in US english."

Samantha raised her eyebrows. "So—you're saying that whoever composed these blackmail letters is a British subject, or reads British magazines?"

O'Malley took a quick sip of his beer. "I think someone high up, in either the US government, the Military, or one of the information-gathering entities like the CIA, could have been involved in a plot to assassinate the President. It makes perfect sense to me—President Lewis was the most unpopular leader in all the history of the White House. There are dozens of people who probably wanted to knock him off."

"But it would be like looking for a needle in a haystack," said Lucas.

O'Malley leaned forward. "Not if you have the right contacts. I know someone who might be able to help us."

Samantha looked doubtful. "Do we really want to get involved? The FBI are already on

to us for withholding information and someone has tried to kill you, Dillon."

Lucas rubbed his chin. "By what you have
just said, Sam, we are, all three of us, already
involved. I have an idea—we need to disappear
for a while and try to work on finding the perpetrators of the assassination."

"How do we just disappear?" O'Malley
asked.

"I have friends in low places. I know to
whom we can look and how we can hide out in
plain sight."

Samantha put on a knowing smile. "Those
homeless friends of yours?"

"Exactly. It's the only sure way we can
evade detection but still maintain a presence,"
said Lucas.

O'Malley gave it some thought. "I think it's
a brilliant idea. I assume these are the same
homeless people who helped us find Coulson?"

"Right on. They are all anti-establishment so it won't take much for me to convince them to help us."

"What will I do with my hair?" Samantha asked.

Lucas laughed. "Shave it all off, honey."

She shot him a horrified glare. O'Malley added fuel to the fire. "At least you won't have to worry about lice, Sam."

Samantha looked crestfallen. "I've always had my hair, spiky and pink."

"We all have to do what we have to do," said O'Malley.

Samantha closed her eyes and rested her head on O'Malley's shoulder. He felt flattered that she seemed drawn to him and he placed his arm around her shoulder.

"Oh, buck up, Samantha. The homeless women will give you a complete new persona— you may even like it," said Lucas.

O'Malley removed his arm from around Samantha's shoulders and removed a cell phone from his pocket. "I need to make a call."

He keyed in a number and waited. An automated voice told him to hold on as the line was busy. He offered a brief explanation to Samantha and Lucas. "This is a an unlisted phone. The FBI will be tracking my old number."

When the line freed up O'Malley embarked on a brief discussion and then abruptly hung up.

Lucas and Samantha looked at him expectantly.

"I have spoken to my secretary at the office. She says the director has ordered an APB on the three of us. We need to leave the pub right now—its one of the places they know I frequent."

"Would they be looking for you?—don't they expect to find you dead in your apartment?" Lucas asked.

"I'm sure the thug, who was sent to kill me, has let them know it didn't happen. They will definitely be looking for me and they may even expect us to hook up with each other. How do we get in touch with your friends, Lucas?" said O'Malley.

∞∞

26

A Meeting of concerned Conspirators

Three men and one woman, all with solemn faces, sat around the desk and listened intently to the chairman of the Joint Chiefs. He addressed the FBI director, one of the men who sat opposite him.

"This should never have got this far. How on earth did you get involved with the memory sweep program in the first place?"

The director shifted uncomfortably in this seat. "I know this sounds a bit lame but my deputy, Don Hadley, thought it a good idea. Two young women had been murdered and one of them had written in a diary, regarding a one night stand with Coulson who let slip about an involvement in the assassination plot, to kill the president. I was away at the time and when I heard about the involvement in the sweep, I made Hadley shut it down immediately."

"It appears you acted too late. I understand Hadley didn't know about our initiative but for someone, like this O'Malley, to actually get into Coulson's mind could be highly dangerous," said the chairman.

Angel leaned forward and spoke. "I think you're making a mountain out of a molehill, Peter. I don't see how O'Malley will be able to tie anything together, from what Coulson knew. In fact, beside the letters, Coulson did not have an inkling who was blackmailing him."

"You may be right, Angel, however, I don't believe we can take the chance. The staff of the Institute must be tracked down and eliminated—also this agent O'Malley."

Angel turned to General Leif Hansen. "When you sent the letters, where did you find the material for composing them?"

"I found them in our attic. My late wife's sister, in England, used to send me these English magazines on DIY and model yacht articles."

Angel looked shocked. "Your wife was English?"

"Born and bred. I met her when she came to the States to do her master's degree."

"And you used those magazines?"

"Sure. No one would be able to trace them—I destroyed them all."

"Did you think of the difference in spelling?" Angel asked.

The general looked shocked. "No—I didn't think of that. I doubt whether I used any words which were purely British."

The chairman jumped in. "But you can't be sure. Coulson destroyed the originals but O'-Malley has been inside Coulson's mind and searched the memories relevant to this case. We had better hope he didn't pick up on any

British spelling. If I must say so, Leif, that was a stupid thing to do."

Leif Hansen dropped his chin. "I'm sorry. I guess it just never struck me as important."

The director added his two cents. "We're all in this whether we like it or not. I will see that these three people are all caught and dealt with. I'm sure that little bitch, Pink, downloaded the results of Coulson's memory sweep and O'Malley will have seen the memory in action."

What about the dean?" Hansen asked.

"I doubt whether he knows anything but he was privy to the talk in the lab."

The chairman turned to the FBI director. "We're banking on your action—don't let us down."

"I won't let you down, Mr. Chairman. I have people out everywhere, looking and they won't be able to hide for long. I have issued their identities to passport control and they will not be able to leave the country."

The meeting ended.

*

O'Malley, Lucas and Samantha sat around the small gas heater and warmed themselves. With them were several homeless people. Shanks looked at Samantha with some amusement. "I must say you look quite different from when I first met you this afternoon."

Samantha looked persecuted. "It's not my cup of tea, but I like the earrings."

Her hair, now a dark brown color, lay flat on her head and a new set of earrings festooned both her lobes. The lipstick, instead of her usual bright pink, displayed a provocative purple and her eyebrows, now jet-black instead of white, changed her entire persona. The jeans, faded and torn, with a yellow blouse and heavy woolen sweater, completed the facade. The small silver rings had all been removed.

Lucas felt quite at home. He always retained, throughout his career, a soft spot for the homeless people of New York and but for his love for physics he might well have joined the crowd. He loved the idea of the few responsibilities and lack of priorities, which the homeless people lived with, on a daily basis. He did, however, enjoy the privileges and money that came with his job. Every two weeks he made it a point to make contact with the folk and provide elements of hygiene and toiletry items, sometimes a bottle of bourbon or rum. Shanks treated Lucas as a brother and would make sure the eyes and ears of the New York homeless society would be available to keep the professor and his two friends safe.

O'Malley expressed his gratitude. "I want to thank you and your friends, Shanks, for taking us in and showing us the ropes. Although this is not a lifestyle I would choose, I respect your decision to live this way."

"Any friend of the professor's is a friend of ours, Special Agent. We're usually trying to avoid your kind but we understand the predicament you are in and we want to be of help," answered Shanks.

O'Malley had encouraged Lucas and Samantha to dump their cell phones in case the FBI used them to track their whereabouts. He possessed one more card up his sleeve. Before meeting up with Shanks and his friends O'Malley stopped in at an ATM and withdrew the daily allowance of eight-hundred dollars. With money in hand he purchased three cheap, cell phones, all with unlisted numbers. He needed to communicate with his secretary and with another colleague in the National Security Agency's statistics division. O'Malley knew, the colleague who had accompanied him on several tours of Iraq, twelve years prior would help him, despite the price on his head.

"I need to make a call," said O'Malley. He excused himself and walked to a tree on the edge of the Yankee Stadium grounds, in the Bronx. They were not far from where Bob Coulson's apprehension took place. He knew, by this time of the evening his friend would be at home, where the phones would not be monitored. He put the call through.

"Brent? It's Dillon. I know all hell has broken loose and you've probably heard that the

FBI director want's my guts, but listen to me for two minutes—I need your help."

His friend expressed surprise and reservations at the call but O'Malley cut him short.

"Brent, It's not what you think. There's a conspiracy afoot and its to do with the assassination of the late President Lewis." O'Malley shared the short version of his story and made his request. "You still owe me one from the Iraq days, Brent—I need you to come through for me, big time."

The call ended with O'Malley closing his eyes in the hope his old friend would not let him down and after standing under the tree for another few moments, he moved back to the small group of homeless people.

"How did it go,Dillon," asked Lucas.

"I believe he will come through for us. He owes me one—I saved his bacon in Iraq."

"What exactly did you ask him to do." asked Samantha.

"He is in control of all records at the NSA and is the ideal person to do a search on backgrounds of all the White House staff and our secret agencies. It's a long shot but I'm looking for people of high rank and influence, who are British born, or are married to British subjects."

"That is a tall order but your friend appears to be the right person for the task," said Shanks.

"He said it might take a couple of days. I only have one more phone left," said O'Malley.

"Don't worry about phones—I can get you as many as like, and all unlisted."

"I like your style, Shanks. Maybe, when all this is over I'll join your ranks."

"You would be most welcome, Special Agent."

"I'll join you, sweetie," said Samantha. "Maybe the two of us can hook up and become a team."

"I'm still married, Sam," said O'Malley.

"Not too happily, I believe," she answered.

O'Malley looked away. He felt a pang of regret for his failing marriage and he missed Janet.

Samantha moved close to him and pecked at his cheek. "No pressure, my sweetie."

The others all laughed but O'Malley felt desolate inside. In the space of a few days his wife had left him, he had joined the ranks of the homeless and now a fugitive, he would spend his days on the run from the law.

∞∞

27

Life on the Streets

Life on the streets presented a completely different mindset requirement. O'Malley, Lucas and Samantha found the first few days a real challenge. Not having access to shower and conventional ablution facilities became a pain for Samantha and they all had to get used to erecting their personal facades every morning. Nights found them sleeping in doorways of businesses and local shops. Shanks knew every place available, where they could rest their

heads and it took much willpower for them to overcome the change in circumstances.

One day a group of homeless stood outside a convenience store where Shanks nurtured a relationship with the owner, who saw to it they received day-old meat cuts and week-old bread, twice every week. Another store owner provided milk, tea and sugar on a regular basis. These give-aways didn't come for nothing. Shanks ran a surveillance group, who kept an eye on the outside merchandise and intervened when local ruffians mostly young teenagers, who tried to steal the goods. Shank's homeless group never went hungry.

Hope of his friend coming through for them seemed more remote as the days went by but in the end, patience rewarded them with some promising information. A week after O'Malley's call to his friend in the NSA, he received an answer.

"What do you have for me, Brent?" O'Malley asked.

"There are five possibles who might fit the bill, Dillon. I will give you their names, official appointments and where they work. I can't do anything more for you on this. I already lied to my supervisor as to why I looked into these files."

O'Malley pulled out a small notebook and pen, from his wallet. Two minutes later he thanked his friend and ended the call. The phone, one of the unlisted he purchased earlier ended up, smashed, in a dumpster. He called

Lucas and Samantha over and they walked together to sit under the tree on the outskirts of the Yankee Stadium grounds. From their vantage point they could see anyone who might approach them.

"I've five names. All these people are high ranking officers in the services and all have links to Britain, of some sort, or they have English family members."

Samantha looked dubious. "How are we ever going to find out who might have been involved in an assassination plot?"

O'Malley thought about her question. "I'm not sure yet but we will find a way. I have a gut-feel that one one of these names will strike pay-dirt."

"What information do you have?" Lucas asked.

"I have the names and addresses of our potential conspirators, the place of office and the kin, with a British affiliation. We'll have to work through these with as much dedication to detail as possible. I will buy a cheap laptop and we'll use the wifi available at the many different spots in the city. Sam, you have an eye for detail—I want you to use the internet to glean all available details on these people."

"Aye, aye, my captain."

"Professor, we'll need your penchant for organizing details and concepts into understandable data, which we can use to eliminate or include in the final synopsis."

"I'll do my best, Dillon, but perhaps you should think of acquiring two laptops instead of just one. I'll be able to collate our data better on my own computer."

"I'll do that—I have about four hundred dollars left. I believe Shanks knows a guy who fixes older computers and sells them cheaply."

"Why don't you want to share with me? You're looking down on my new-found status as a homeless waif?" Samantha asked.

Lucas laughed. "As one homeless person to another I'm putting in a complaint to the vagrancy committee—you need a shower."

Samantha glared at him and lunged out with her fist, striking him on the shoulder. "At least my teeth are clean, moron. You still have the last two meals stuck between your incisors."

O'Malley shook his head and smiled. "When you two kids are finished arguing about incidentals, we have work to do."

They laughed and joined the group, sitting around the gas heater.

*

In a back alley, lit by a single street light, Samantha worked diligently to gather information from the internet. The WiFi connection came from the backend of an all-night cafe, where she huddled closely with Lucas and O'-Malley. In a small alcove, near the backdoor the backlit screen of the laptop, illuminating her surroundings.

"The first person on your list is Dana Avery. She is a senior press coordinator in the White House and lives in Washington DC. Her personal bio states she was educated in London and moved to the United States at the age of twenty-one. She is married and now forty-six years old. Her entire family lives in DC."

Lucas recorded the data in a spreadsheet on his laptop. "Does she take frequent trips back to England?" O'Malley asked.

"I'll need to check her face book page." Samantha negotiated the internet search and accessed Avery's face book, with ease.

"How did you gain access so easily?" Lucas asked.

"Trade secret, my love. It shows she has recently visited Fiji and Hawaii. It will be difficult to tell if she has been back to England in recent years."

"Okay I've recorded the information. Let's move onto the next person," said Lucas.

O'Malley heard the sound of a car trolling along the alleyway and saw a bright spotlight illuminating the back entrances—a police patrol doing a routine check on business premises.

"Quickly, we must get out of sight before that patrol car arrives opposite this doorway," whispered O'Malley. Unfortunately no escape route availed itself to them and the car pulled up to the sidewalk with the three fugitives in full view. The laptops were stuffed into a trashcan which conveniently sat at the back-door.

A patrol officer stepped out of the car followed by his buddy, a short, petite black woman. "What's going on here?"

The officer's voice, a white male, sounded gruff.

Lucas stepped forward and spoke, shielding O'Malley and Samantha from view as much as he could. "We're just looking for a place to spend the night, officer."

The patrolman shone his flashlight on the threesome and observed them for a few seconds. "Homeless?" He asked.

"Unfortunately, yes, Sir."

"Well, you can't sleep here. Can I see some ID, please?"

Lucas stepped closer and handed the officer a fake ID which Shanks set up for each of them. The policewoman stepped forward and took the ID and scrutinized it for a few moments. "How long have you been homeless? I know a lot of the people and I've never seen any of you," she asked.

"We've been around for years—we're a part of Shank's group," said Lucas.

The patrolman smiled. "Oh yes, I know Shanks well—where would you normally find him?"

The officer did not seem totally convinced and appeared to be probing for a lie. "We usually congregate close to the Yankee Stadium, around a small gas heater, when its cool like this."

"So why are you here?" The woman asked.

"We were helping the owner with eyes on the outside stock until seven pm. He gave us some food and we decided to eat it here at the backdoor. It's warm and cosy so we thought to stay the night."

"You best find a shelter, Mr. Strong. You and and your friends can't stay here tonight."

"Of course, Officer. We often stay in the Bluebird family Shelter—it's not far from here. We'll make our way there."

The policewoman handed the ID back and they both nodded. "Best be moving on," she said.

"Thanks for your understanding," said Lucas.

The two officers got back into the car and drove off, leaving the three gaping after them. "Whew. That was close," said O'Malley.

"We really need to be more vigilant," said Lucas.

"The police must have standing orders, regarding the three of us. I think the mention of Shanks and your knowledge of the Bluebird Shelter, averted any suspicions they might have had," said O'Malley.

"We need to keep an open path for quick escapes at all times," said Samantha. She dug into the trash can and produced the two laptops.

They decided to move back through the system of alleyways, to the Stadium area, where they usually slept.

*

In the morning, after a community breakfast with Shanks and the group, work on the list resumed at a new WiFi hotspot near a deli.

The next three names did not raise any eyebrows and O'Malley began to think they may not be able to find what they were looking for. The last name, however, set a fire, in O'Malley's mind. "General, Leif Hansen. I know that name but where did I hear of him?"

Samantha grabbed O'Malley's fingers. "I remember from the record of Coulson's memory sweep. Hansen was Coulson's commanding officer in Afghanistan. He's the one who stood up for Coulson over the friendly-fire incident."

"You're absolutely correct, Sam. Good memory recall, girl," said Lucas.

O'Malley beamed all over. "We have something here, at last."

"Hansen would have had access to Coulson's file. Something happened during the gunfight that obviously threw suspicion on Coulson's actions, as a leader. Perhaps someone saw, or overheard what Coulson did, to cause his men to fire on those Canadian soldiers and Hansen took care of the issue," said Samantha.

"Grounds for blackmailing Coulson at a later date, or having him in pocket," said O'Malley.

"What is his designation?" O'Malley asked.

Samantha called up the general's bio and read off a few lines.

"General Leif Hansen has risen to new heights since his command in Afghanistan. He is currently the Commandant of the Marine

Corps and is a member of the Joint Chiefs of Staff."

O'Malley whistled. "Big fish, indeed. I guess he is stationed at the Pentagon?"

"Correct. Here's the most interesting fact, though—his late wife, Erica Hansen, was a British subject and they met while she was doing a master's degree in the US. She died two years ago from cancer. He has been single ever since."

Samantha's fingers rattled over the keys and a face book page popped up. "It looks as though the general took over her face book page after her death. Look at all the contact with family in Britain. It's still ongoing—but this is what we are looking for; a posting giving thanks to her sister for the magazines on DIY, sent via post. It looks as if he receives them from his wife's sister, on a regular basis."

"Why wouldn't he just use DIY mags from the USA. God knows we have plenty publications here?" Lucas queried.

"This particular publication group deals with model yachts—maybe thats the reason.

Perhaps he's into english yachts and sailing," said Samantha.

"It seems a reasonable theory. These are possibly the magazines used to compose the blackmail letters," said O'Malley.

Samantha trolled further through the postings and confirmed the theory. "Here's a picture of him holding up a model yacht for a photo. I'm bang on."

Lucas chuckled. "you go bang quite often."

"Shut up, you fossilized embryo." She reached out, grabbed him around the neck with her arm and pummeled his forehead.

O'Malley didn't want the glory of the moment to melt down into insults so he stood and made to return to the group.

"I'll leave the two of you to sort each other out. I'm going to brainstorm a way to expose Leif Hansen. I'm sure he's not working alone, so we'll have to be extremely careful.

∞∞

28

A Need for Intimacy

O'Malley's thoughts ranged far and wide as he tried to get some sleep. The small group lay on assortments of old, worn mattresses and blankets with cardboard ground sheets under them. Samantha chose, as she always did, to lie between O'Malley and Lucas, her petite body wrapped in an old woolen blanket, a gift from one of the homeless women. She made it a point to lie as close to O'Malley as she could, without touching any part of his body. The overhang of the stadium's bleachers stretched out above them and afforded a certain amount of protection from the elements, in particular the cool night air. The occasional shower would bring a frosty mist and the people would pull the blankets over their heads, thankful for the overhang.

O'Malley's mind stretched in two directions. An excitement mixed with some trepidation, with regards to exposing the conspiracy, wrestled with the pain of his failed family relationship. He still loved Janet and longed to overcome the sadness in his heart of a daughter lost, to bring closure to his failure in the prime responsibility of his parenthood. The call to duty remained strong, despite the rejection by his peers over the Hadley debacle and he still believed in the memory sweep, as a mighty tool for crime resolution.

With his thoughts careening wildly over the map a sudden touch on his ankle burst the bubble of intense contemplation. He lay with his back to Samantha and became aware of her presence close up behind him. He turned his head and shoulders enough to see her face in the semi-illumination of a nearby streetlamp. She used the tip of a toe to stroke the back of his calf and he had no illusions as to her motives. The need for intimacy screamed at him. He could feel the pull in his loins and his heart lurched in its ribcage, enough to make him turn over and face her. She drew closer and kissed his lips lightly. The sensation coursed through him like a wild fire and for a brief moment he felt out of control.

O'Malley's thoughts turned to his relationship with his wife and he could see Janet's face clearly—tears streamed down her flushed cheeks and she gazed at him with pain in her eyes. His son, Steven, also looked at him with an undeniable incredulity. A cough from Lucas, graveled through the intense atmosphere between them, sending a clear message of disapproval. Whether this came by design or in slumber, O'Malley would never know. The moment became too much for him. He jumped up, threw the blanket off and stalked away to the tree, where he sat with his back against the trunk, to cool his rising libido. Samantha didn't move and neither did Lucas. The thought filtered through to his conscious mind —did he just have a dream?

After an hour O'Malley returned to his bed. Samantha lay facing the opposite way, closer to Lucas, who lay with his back toward her. He lay down, pulled the blanket over his head and fell asleep.

The first rays of sunshine started at about 5:30 a.m. and the homeless community started to rise, to face the day. The gas heater drew some of the group to its warm radiation while others still lingered with blankets over their heads. O'Malley cranked open an eyelid and thoughts of the night's adventure came with alacrity. Did he dream it? The feeling of Samantha's soft lips on his, still lingered in his mind and he surmised it had to have been real. How would he face her?

"Feeling okay, sweetie?" Samantha's voice floated toward him against the backdrop of all the city noises.

"Yeah, I'm good, Sam. A bit tired—still trying to wake up."

"Did I frighten you, last night?" She said it with such innocence.

He lied. "No, no. Not at all. My mind was just all over the map, is all."

"I know you have a lot to deal with, hon, but don't let it all get to you. Auntie Sam's got your back."

He stared at her and wondered if she understood anything of what he faced. "We have some decisions to make. I've given the conspiracy some thought and as soon as we have finished with breakfast, I would like you and Lucas to sit with me, to do some planning."

With breakfast out of the way O'Malley called Shanks, Samantha and Lucas to sit with him under the tree. Shanks understood their plight and offered the group's help in what ever way O'Malley required it.

"We need to find some evidence of the magazines used by Hansen for the composition of the blackmail letters. My guess is he will have disposed of them into his garbage, for removal to the nearest waste disposal site, to his home. He could also have taken them there himself."

"We're not so acquainted with the DC waste sites but I have some strong contacts in the general area," said Shanks.

O'Malley nodded. "The waste site closest to where the general lives is the Fort Totten Solid Waste Disposal station. It's on Puerto Rica Avenue—do you have any contacts in this area?"

"Yes, we do. It's a bit of a long shot but the material often backs up for weeks before being processed in most of these disposal sites. We may have a chance. I will make contact with a friend who might know one of the employees," answered Shanks.

"Great—thanks, Shanks. Excuse the pun."

"What do we do in the meantime?" Samantha asked.

"We travel to DC and stake out the general's home. We see who visits him and who he visits. I will get hold of my friend in the NSA again, to see if he is willing to give us any further help. If I can track down the general's itinerary it would be helpful."

"I have some very good people who will keep up surveillance on the general's coming and going," said Shanks. "I will need some change for the subway if you have any, Dillon."

O'Malley dug around in his pockets and hauled out some change. "Let's get going, then."

Shanks moved back to the group, issued some instructions and then left for the nearest subway station, where he could catch a train to Washington DC.

"I guess we should also make a plan to get to Washington. I have twenty-eight dollars left, how much do you both have?" O'Malley asked.

Samantha looked at him with her large blue eyes. "A fiver."

Lucas felt in all his trouser pockets and came up with two twenty dollar bills. "This is all I have left."

They gathered up their few belongings, said goodbye to the group and followed in Shanks's footsteps.

Later in the day they met with Shanks in a secluded vicinity of Virginia, where a few of the high-ranking officers who worked at the Pentagon, lived. Shanks introduced three of his contacts to them, who would keep an eye on general Hansen's home and report what they observed. A suitable place near Arlington cemetery, chosen by one of Shank's contacts, would provide a place for them to sleep.

Their new home away from home, turned out to be a bus-shelter which received no traffic after 11:00 pm at night. Police rarely ever showed up to check the facility and he deemed it safe for them to hunker down.

"I want to send the general a message," said O'Malley.

"What about?" Samantha asked.

"I want to spook him into some action. He needs to know we're onto him and we have proof he is the blackmailer. I would also say we know others are involved in the conspiracy, which will cause them to meet for a talk."

"What good will it do us to spook them? We could never be privy to their meeting, which would most likely be at the Pentagon."

"That is where I intend to gain my NSA contact's help," said O'Malley.

"You are going to ask him to report on the general's itinerary?" Samantha exclaimed.

"If I can twist his arm. All events and meetings involving staff in the military, are recorded for security purposes. They will have the names of visitors and members."

"Clever," said Samantha. "Let's hope you can convince your friend to do his magic."

One of Shanks's contacts gave them the address of an all-night internet cafe in the area where O'Malley could type a letter on his laptop and print it off. By 11:30 p.m. they arrived back at the bus shelter, ready for some shut-eye.

Little did they know a night of terror awaited them.

*

General Leif Hansen waited nervously for the others to arrive. Opposite him sat an unsmiling chairman of the joint chiefs. A few minutes later the FBI director arrived with the fourth member of the conspiracy—Angel. They took their seats and waited for the chairman to speak.

"So what is this letter you've received, Leif?"

The general produced a folded piece of paper from inside his tunic and spread it out on the desk. The chairman picked it up and read the contents.

"What proof could they have?" He asked.

"They say a flash drive exists with Coulson's memories on it and there is a reference to the blackmail letters." The general's voice shook with anxiety.

"They would never be able to produce it as evidence," said the FBI director.

'They say they have found the original magazines at the dump, from which the words were cut for the letters. These magazines will be traceable to me."

"We have no evidence they've found the old magazines. You got rid of them some time ago, didn't you?" Angel asked.

"I did, however, there has been a huge backup of garbage at the disposal site. It's possible the magazines were not destroyed."

"Good God, man. Please don't tell me this is going bring us down," shouted the chairman.

Angel remained calm and voiced her opinion. "It's possible but not probable. I assume this suspended, special agent of yours, is behind this. We need to find them quickly."

The director winced. "I have an APB out on all three of them—O'Malley, professor Wheeler and Pink, but we have not been able to locate them as yet. They have somehow managed to stay out of sight."

"I'm willing to bet they have gone to ground —but in a certain way," answered Angel.

"What do you mean?"

She inclined her head and raised her eyebrows. "They have probably gone homeless and are living on the streets."

General Hansen concurred. "It makes sense."

The FBI director stood to his feet. "There's no time to waste. I'll get some of my most trusted men to do a search of the places where the homeless sleep. We'll pick them up for sure. I would think they're in Washington by now, observing as much of Leif's movements, as possible."

"And what will you do when you find them? The chairman asked.

"I'll make sure we get the evidence, if it indeed exists. After that they will simply disappear."

"This is on you and Leif—the two of you better make this right. We are banking on it."

The meeting ended and the director, with general Hansen, left the the chairman's office. Angel stayed for a final word.

"We had better make a plan with our two comrades. They've bungled things badly and I don't want to go down because of their stupidity."

∞∞

29

Caught Unawares

At one am in the morning Samantha awoke from a deep sleep. She needed to pee and cursed the fact she had imbibed two glasses of water before turning in. Lucas and O'Malley slept on their thin, roll-out mattresses each man with a thick woolen blanket, for cover.

She threw off her blanket and crept silently to the back of the shelter where several bushes lined the perimeter of a park. A large bush provided good protection from vehicle's which passed by on occasion. What a life, she thought. This type of living took some adjustment, to every aspect of one's daily routine. She squatted behind the bush and relieved herself . When her ablution ended she stood to walked back to the shelter but the noise of a vehicle caught her attention. A dark SUV pulled up. The driver must have coasted the final thirty, or forty yards before applying his brakes, to stop adjacent to the shelter. Samantha froze and watched from the confines of her hiding place as three figures alighted the SUV and with stealth, approached the two men sleeping in the shelter.

She wanted to scream but intuition begged her silence. She watched in horror as the three figures surrounded O'Malley and Lucas. They reached down to the two sleeping figures and without ceremony, yanked the men to their feet. Both Lucas and O'Malley, taken by surprise, could only shake their heads in an attempt to bring their thoughts to focus on the apprehension.

"Finally we have caught up with you. O'-Malley," said one of the men. The three, dressed in military fatigues, pummeled their catch with slaps and punches. Lucas tried to fight back but with his mind still in a fog his efforts produced a few chuckles from the men in fatigues. Samantha knew she would need to leave, or be caught. She silently melted into the park area to hide. Nearby, a stream gurgled along a manmade waterway, where the path meandered over a small bridge to continue on into the park, through a group of trees.

Samantha dived under the bridge and remained there, her heart pounding like a sledgehammer. She could hear the voices clearly.

One of the men addressed their two prisoners. "There appears to have been a third person sleeping here—I assume the infamous, Miss Pink. Where is she?"

"Lucas spoke in a shaky voice. She must have got up for a pee."

The man, the leader of the threesome, spoke with a terse note, to one of his underlings. "See if you can find her."

The man left the group and ran behind the shelter, to peer amongst the bushes. When he came up with nothing he ventured further afield, a small flashlight clutched in his hand. After ten minutes of fruitless search he returned to the shelter.

"She's gone. There are a thousand places to hide and she may have kept running."

"No matter, we have the two main culprits. We'll get her soon enough. Let's go."

They forced Lucas and O'Malley into the SUV and drove off at speed.

Samantha came out of her hiding place, her mind in a whirl. She did not know where Shanks and his contacts bedded down for the night but she knew one of the group would be watching the general's home in the morning and should be able to tell her where the homeless panhandler might be. She perceived Luke and O'Malley would be in the greatest of danger and normal FBI rules, or protocols, would not apply. These enforcers would not be able to explain to the rest of the world why they had apprehended her two friends and would more than likely, force the whereabouts of the evidence, out of them.

*

The SUV sped through the deserted streets to a destination known to the captors. O'Malley and Lucas both felt sick to their stomachs.

The only consolation being Samantha's escape. But what could she do in the face of military and FBI might? She might be able to make contact with Shanks again, but in all truth, there appeared little anyone would be able to do. O'Malley and Lucas would not be able to hold onto the flash drive evidence when their captors submitted them to rigorous torture. The only light at the end of the tunnel for them, lay in the possibility of Shanks's people finding the magazines—a long shot, in consideration of the fact they may have been disposed of by the waste station.

The flash drive presented some problems. The technology could be discredited and made un-admissible in a court of law. They arrived at their destination and O'Malley could only pick up the sound of water, docks, or a waterfront—perhaps the Potomac River. The captors hustled the two men out of the SUV and through a door into a dimly lit hallway. Another door appeared and they found themselves in a room, with one lightbulb in the center of the ceiling. A tall man, whom O'Malley recognized as an

FBI agent, stood over them as they lay on the floor with their hands cuffed.

"Thought you could get away with all this, didn't you, O'Malley?"

O'Malley said nothing. The man leading the interrogation, known for his ruthlessness and brutal approach, glared at him with hostility.

"There is a package we are looking for. A flash drive, to start with. I believe you know where it is?"

O'Malley stared him in the eye. "I don't know what you're talking about, Richardson."

Richardson's boot shot out and caught the special agent in the ribs. O'Malley doubled over in pain, collapsed and took on the fetal position.

"Let me jog your memory, O'Malley. You, your friend and the girl, recorded a session of Coulson's memory sweep and then deleted it from the computer's hard drive. We're certain of its existence. Save yourself a lot of trouble and tell me where it has been hidden."

"Go jump in a lake, Richardson. Do you know you're aiding and assassination conspiracy?"

"I don't know anything about a conspiracy, O'Malley—we're under orders and we are loyal to the FBI code. You are a renegade and you will pay the price. Maybe we will prove you and your two friends are part of this conspiracy."

O'Malley shut his mouth and continued to stare into Richardson's eyes. The interrogator lifted O'Malley to his feet and swung his fist, which caught the special agent on the bridge of the nose. Blood spattered and the two other captors chuckled.

"Well see how brave you are when we start on your friend, here."

O'Malley's stomach lurched as Richardson lifted Lucas onto his feet and smashed an iron fist into Lucas's mouth. A tooth spilled out and Lucas fainted. He flopped in Richardson's grip and the interrogator punched him several more times until O'Malley relented.

"Okay, Richardson—you win." He came to a swift decision. The sweep record might not be admissible in legal proceedings and he considered it as more of a back up. The real evidence lay in the location of the magazines. He would now have to bank on Shanks's people finding the evidence and staying out of sight. He doubted the assassins knew about Shanks's involvement in the accumulation of information.

"The flash drive is hidden in a lab wall-socket, amongst the cables. You will not find it without parting those cables and digging for it."

Richardson smiled. He picked up his cell phone from the small desk in the corner and made a call.

*

Samantha made her way to the general's home in Virginia. It took some time but with the aid of a map, she easily found her way. On arrival she walked to a kiddie's play-park on the corner of the block and lit up a cigarette. Ten minutes later she noticed a shabbily dressed person, who shuffled along the sidewalk, in impersonation of an elderly bum. She recognized him from the previous day. He recognized her.

"What brings you here this morning, Ma'am? Where are the others?"

She told him the story of the night's terror and asked where she could find Shanks.

"He'll be at the Fort Totten Waste Station, searching for those mags."

The man showed her on the map how to get there. "If you got a few dollars you can catch a number four bus at the bottom of this road. It'll taker you right past the Station."

Samantha thanked him and made her way to the bus stop. The number four bus arrived a few minutes later and she got on. She placed a five dollar bill in the driver's outstretched hand. He gave her two dollars change and she took a seat.

Forty minutes later the driver stopped at a shelter and to Samantha's delight, Shanks and two of his people stood behind the structure, talking to each other. She jumped off the bus, rushed up to Shanks and embraced him.

"Whoa, whoa, girl," said Shanks. His surprise showed and he held her at arms length.

"Easy, love. Don't get carried away, now—my girls might get jealous." he chuckled and then saw Samantha's eyes, which registered her angst.

"They've taken Lucas and O'Malley," she blurted.

"Oh no—how did it happen?"

She explained what had transpired earlier that morning and how she, by providence, escaped the clutches of the captors.

"It was the FBI, three of them and they whisked O'Malley and Lucas away in an SUV. There was nothing I could do."

Shanks looked at her with empathy. "We have one consolation," he said. "We've found the magazines—and just in the nick of time. Four FBI police arrived, to case out the joint. I guess they knew we might try to find the evidence. It only proves how desperate the conspirators are, to cover this up."

"This is great news. We'll more than likely lose the flash drive when those villains resort to torturing our two boys," said Samantha.

Shanks rubbed his chin. "We have to make contact with the conspirators, somehow and let them know we have the magazines."

"What will we do? Make a trade?"

Shanks considered the question. "No—we can't do that. If they get the magazines we are up the creek without the old proverbial paddle and they may still kill the boys."

"What are we going to do, then?" Samantha asked. She could feel the bile rising in her throat.

"We will make contact and tell them the evidence is in a senior CIA officer's hands. The chips are up for the conspirators. If they kill O'Malley and Lucas, it will only deepen the hole they have dug for themselves.

"It's a gamble, but sounds logical."

"I can't see any other way out," said Shanks. The sound of a cellphone ringing caught their ears and they all jumped. The ringtone came from O'Malley's bag which Samantha had collected from the shelter after the incident. She hastily opened the bag and pulled out the phone.

"Hello?"

"Where's Dillon?" asked the voice.

"This is Samantha Pink. I'm one of Dillon's associates involved with the investigation. The FBI have caught Dillon and professor Wheeler. We're figuring out how to get them back—we do have the evidence we need to expose one of the conspirators."

The voice remained silent for a few moments. "I have some more info that might be helpful," said the stranger.

"Anything to help get O'Malley and my friend, Lucas, back," she said.

The man would not give his name but she knew this to be O'Malley's contact at the NSA.

"The chairman of the joint Chiefs had a meeting with three other people, yesterday. They were general Hansen, the director of the FBI and a woman called, Angel—I don't know who she is. This is all I can tell you."

"Thanks. You've been a tremendous help," said Samantha.

"Good luck," said the stranger. He ended the call.

∞∞

30

Nowhere to Hide

The Chairman of the Joint Chiefs surveyed his three fellow conspirators.

"Good work on apprehending O'Malley and his one companion. I assume you will eventually catch the woman as well?"

The FBI director nodded. "There isn't much she can do and we'll eventually find her. She will be silenced. We have the flash drive and there is no evidence the magazines were ever found."

"We don't know if that is true. The flash drive is evidence which they know may not be accepted in court—the magazines would be the only other way their case against you could be made," said the chairman. He looked directly at Hansen who turned paler than he had been on entering the meeting.

Angel sat with legs crossed and hands folded. "Do you have a plan if they did find those magazines, Leif?"

Hansen looked at the ceiling. "I will take care of it. They'll never get to me and hence they will not get to the three of you."

"You are prepared to do what it takes?" The director asked.

"I am prepared, yes—but there is no certainty that these people are not aware of other's being involved in the conspiracy."

"I guess there isn't much more to discuss. You need to keep us informed, Leif. They will most certainly be onto you if those magazines have been found."

An aide knocked on the door and waited for the chairman to notice her.

"Stella?" said the chairman.

"Sir, there is an envelope addressed to you. It was delivered a few moments ago by a scruffy man who insisted you see the contents."

She walked in and handed the envelope to the chairman. He took it and looked at the handwritten instructions on the front.

"This is unusual," he said.

He opened the envelope and pulled out a bunch of photocopies. After perusing them he flung them onto the desktop for the others to see. They all craned forward and scrutinized the papers.

"Oh no," said the director.

Leif Hansen fell back into his chair and looked as though a heart attack might overtake him. Angel, the only one to keep composure said, "I'm out of this. I don't know how these people found out about us. Some one informed them. I do know, however, my name is only registered as a visitor with the name of, 'Angel.'"

The chairman pulled a handkerchief from his pocket to wipe his brow. "You were the main instigator in this, Angel. You can't just pull out and think they won't track you down."

"You take care of yourselves but I'm out of here. Unlike you three, I have an escape plan."

Angel stood and to their astonishment, walked out of the office, down the hall and out of a side door to the carpark.

The FBI director looked at the chairman and stood to his feet. "I'm going home to do what must be done."

General Leif Hansen pulled out a revolver from his tunic pocket and shot himself in the mouth. The chairman sat immobilized, with wide, open eyes. He shouted for his aide and a group of people close by, came at the run. The sound of the shot carried far down the corridors of the Pentagon building and more people crept to the office door for a quick look.

The general's brains lay spattered over the backrest of his chair and his body lay slumped over to one side, still in a sitting position. The chairman sat in shock, wild eyed as the security rushed in, to secure the office.

Angel got into a car, drove toward the small apartment in Manhattan and on arrival gathered up a suitcase, already packed. A passport was pulled from a drawer and haste made toward the J. F Kennedy airport.

*

O'Malley looked at his persecutor. Richardson's face showed no emotion after receiving a call from the director. Lucas lay unconscious on the ground, his mouth and nose, leaking blood onto the floor.

Richardson put down his phone and walked over to O'Malley, who expected the worse.

"Turn around," he said.

O'Malley obliged and presented his cuffed wrists. A surge of hope flowed through him.

"You and your friend are free to go. Just remember—I meant no disrespect. I was just following orders."

He opened the cuffs and did the same for the professor.

"Where are you going?" O'Malley asked.

"Back to the office to report. You do what you have to do." he beckoned to his chums and they left the room. O'Malley stood in a quandary. He couldn't find any stable grounds for believing his ears. Was he dreaming, still unconscious or asleep? He pinched himself and felt the pain. No—it had been real. He knelt down and shook Lucas on the shoulder.

"Wake up, Luke, wake up."

The professor took a little while to surface. He sat up and grabbed his head before flopping onto his back. "My head and face hurt like the devil."

"We are free to leave, when you feel able," said O'Malley.

This shook the professor out of his fogginess. "How do you mean?"

"I don't really know but I think Sam might have had something to do with it."

He explained Richardson's strange behavior after receiving a call. "We need to find Sam

and Shanks. I think they may be able to fill us in on what's happened."

"Let's get out of here, then," said Lucas.

They helped each other out of the building and into the street. O'Malley's ears appeared to have heard the correct sounds which gave him the inkling of their geographical position. They found themselves at a waterfront property on what seemed to be the Potomac river.

"Samantha may have my bag and there are still two phones in it. We need to find a call box and I'll see if I can raise her," said O'Malley.

They came across an outdoor phone cubicle, attached to a pole. O'Malley felt around in his pockets for change. He found three quarters and hoped it would be enough. The telephone numbers of the unlisted phones differed only by the last digit for each one, making it easy to remember. He slipped the coins into the machine and dialed a number. It rang for a full minute, before Samantha answered.

"Sam," shouted O'Malley. What did you do? —we're free."

"Dillon? Is this really you? Thank God it worked."

"What worked?" O'Malley asked.

Samantha told him of how she escaped and met up with Shanks. She shared how they found the magazines, in piles awaiting incineration, moments before the FBI moved in and how they made copies of the pages which were used in the composing of the blackmail letters.

O'Malley shook his head in a daze. "So you sent someone to deliver photocopies? How did you know the chairman of the Joint Chiefs was involved?"

She shared about the call from his contact at the NSA.

"Thank God for Brent," said O'Malley. I knew he would come through for us."

"Where are you," asked Samantha.

O'Malley took the folded map out of his pocked and spread it on a bench, near the payphone. He found their location quickly and

told her. "I think we can safely return to our homes. It doesn't look as though we're on the FBI's most wanted list, anymore."

*

Five hours later O'Malley, Samantha and Lucas arrived back at the place where the Bentley awaited them. They all felt they wanted three things: a good shower, a solid meal and sleep. Samantha's love for Lucas showed.

"Poor baby. Your looks have been altered a little but you're still my fossilized embryo."

He looked at O'Malley, who shook his head. They drove to Lucas's home and decided to stay there for the night, until they received news as to the conspirators fate. After each took long showers, which emptied the hot-water tank, the three ordered in Pizza and Lucas opened a bottle of wine. He turned on the TV and they caught up on the latest news.

...tragedy struck the Pentagon this morning when a four-star general, General leif Hansen, a veteran of the marine core and its leader, shot himself in front of the chairman of the Joint Chiefs. It is said, a person referred to as Angel, walked out of the meeting minutes before the general shot himself. Also involved was the director of the FBI, who refused to comment on the situation. Several documents strewn on the chairman's desk were taken into the CIA's possession and there are rumors of a conspiracy which involved the assassination of President Lewis. The chairman of the Joint Chiefs, General Hansen, the FBI director and the mystery person are said to have been involved in the plot to assassinate the President. The two men have been taken into custody but there is no sign of the person called, Angel....

The three stared at each other in disbelief. Their mission to expose the conspirators had been successful. O'Malley grinned. "Well, doesn't that just top it off neatly?"

Lucas looked thoughtful. "I'm still wondering about the person called Angel."

*

Angel stood in line at the counter to purchase a oneway ticket to Argentina. Money from a secret account awaited in Rio. The plane would be leaving in forty minutes. After purchasing a ticket Angel walked down the corridor toward the gate, allocated to the aircraft.

Twenty minutes later the boarding for Rio started and Angel stood with the rest of the passengers. On arrival at the checkin counter the airport official looked at the boarding pass and smiled. "Have a good trip Mrs. Lewis."

∞∞

EPILOGUE

The dean sat in his chair and laughed. "So, Sam. You experienced the rougher side of life. How did you manage living out under the stars?"

Samantha grinned. It was great. I have a newfound appreciation for the homeless. Had it not been for them we would have been done for."

"I kind of liked your false identity," said Lucas. "You're back to looking like a goofy tooth fairy again."

She shot out of her chair and landed in his lap. "And you look like an overstuffed hippy on steroids."

"I like the way I look," he said. "At least I look human."

The dean shook his head and turned his eyes toward the ceiling. "I have some news for the two of you. Your research and experimentation with the memory sweeper has been nominated for best scientific advancement of the year."

Lucas stood up and dislodged Samantha who caught the side of the chair before she hit the ground.

"That's wonderful. Do you think it will land us a nobel prize," asked Lucas.

"There's a rumor of it," said the dean.

Lucas grabbed Samantha by the hand and they ran down the corridor together, toward the lab. In wonderment they entered their scientific shrine and stared at the particle accelerator, with its connecting harnesses.

Lucas grabbed Samantha and pulled her to him.

"There's something I've been meaning to do," he said.

Her eyes fluttered and she tried to act dumb. "And what would that be?"

He stared into her eyes and positioned his lips for a kiss. She closed her eyes and lifted her mouth to meet his. At that moment the class bell jingled loudly, an indication to students that classes for the day had ended.

Lucas looked at her and said. "I've just remembered something." He turned away from her to the computer and sat down at the desk. She stood with her lips still puckered and eyes closed. "Lucas—don't you dare. Get back here to me."

*

O'Malley unlocked the front door of his apartment and walked into silence. His thoughts swirled around in his mind. Thoughts of Janet's soft lips and her skin, smooth to the touch, and he missed her. He kept on seeing a vision of his son Steven, who looked at him with contempt for a farther who always put his job first. How would he ever make it up to them. He needed to get closure on his daughter's death, before he lost the family altogether. He needed to make amends for his absenteeism and the constant flow of negativity that occupied his thoughts. He would call Janet.

He walked into the living room and almost fainted with fright. Janet rushed at him and threw her arms around his neck. His son also joined in the group hug.

"I've been so worried about you, my darling, she said."

O'Malley couldn't find words. He knew he needed to share everything that had happened to him. To confide in their capacity to hold his secrets and start afresh. He would battle his demons and win. They sank down on the settee in a tangle of arms and legs.

O'Malley knew that all would be well.

The End

More Books by Colin Setterfield

The Helium-3 Conspiracy

Subduction Zone

Love Sweat tears

*The A-Mortal Gene

*The habitat Relocation Project

*The Beautiful Planet

Merlin's War.   SpeciaL Agent O'Malley

The Omega File. Special Agent O'Malley

Operation Terra Firma. Special Agent O'-Malley

www.ingramcontent.com/pod-product-compliance
Lightning Source LLC
Chambersburg PA
CBHW030621250626
47154CB00006B/1875